Purr-Fect Pitch

Award Winning Romantic Comedy

Carolyn Wren

Carolyn Wren

National Library of Australia Cataloguing-in-publication data:

ISBN (p) 978-1-7643181-3-6 978-1-7643181-5-0 (e)
978-1-7643181-4-3 Purr-Fect Pitch/Carolyn Wren

To all the cat's who've brought such joy into my life.
And to my wonderful cat loving, music loving
husband, who inspired the character of Devlin.

CONTENTS

Chapter One

Ringing.

An insistent, continuous, ringing dragged Dev from a brain-dead sleep. Stifling a groan, he reached across and thumped the alarm clock. The sound continued. Shaking off the groggy confusion, he dragged himself out of bed, as the cacophony appeared to be someone leaning on the doorbell.

Dev barrelled down the stairs, almost succumbing to a broken neck when an impatient Siamese wound herself between his feet.

"Hang on, Carmen. I'll feed you in a sec."

Damn, his head was throbbing. Who the hell came up with the idea of having a massive party the night before his birthday, therefore consigning the actual *day* of his birth to hangover territory?

Oh, yeah... that would be his brothers. The moment he laid eyes on them again, they were toast.

Dev yanked open the front door. Bright sunlight seared his retinas with stunning accuracy, shocking his brain into full consciousness. Haloed within the blinding light was a kitten. Or more accurately, a woman dressed as a kitten, with a black leotard clinging to killer curves, furry ears pinned to light blond curls and whiskers drawn on porcelain pale cheeks.

To add to the surreal image, she began to sing.

"*I'm a tiger, I'm a tiger...*"

Her voice was a sexy hum of sound tingling along his spine. Intrigued, but confused, Dev held up his hand. "I think you have the wrong house."

"No, I don't," she took a deep breath. "*I'm a tiger, I'm a...*"

She paused when his hand rose again.

"I'm sorry, either I'm still asleep or...?" he left the question open.

Her soft, but stubborn chin kicked upwards. "I'm a singing telegram."

"Who on earth—?" He didn't even finish the sentence. His damn brothers were definitely toast.

"Alright, I'll play along, why a cat?"

"You love cats."

Dev would have argued, except at that precise moment, Evita, his Persian, curled around his ankles, demanding attention, or breakfast, or both. He picked her up. She purred like a freight train against his face.

The other kitten, the human one, raised a brow. "May I continue?"

Inclining his head, he encouraged her.

"*I'm a tiger...*"

This time when his hand rose, she huffed out a breath and glared at him. "What now?"

"Tigers have stripes."

Small dainty hands settled on her hips. "Your point?"

"You don't." He gestured to her outfit.

"They didn't have a striped leotard costume at the office." Despite the professional smile, her tone could have frozen a volcano.

His little songstress kitten had claws. Dev resisted the urge to grin. "Then why are you singing about a tiger?"

"I-did-not-choose-the-song." Each word was succinct.

"Aah, it's because I like cats."

"You *love* cats," she corrected.

"And you know this how?"

"It's written all over your face." Her sky-blue eyes danced with mischief.

Something about it alerted him. Dev glanced at the hallway mirror. The words, *'I Love Cats'* were written in black marker across his forehead. Knowing his evil younger siblings, it was permanent ink.

He blew out a long-suffering breath. "Do you have brothers?"

"No."

"I envy you." Dev scrubbed at the writing. As he suspected, it didn't even smudge.

She cleared her throat in a not-so-subtle hint. "I do need to finish this song, as I have several other bookings today."

He turned back to face her. "I have a question."

"*Another* question, you mean?"

God, she was feisty, and sassy, and gorgeous. "You're exceptionally talented. Why are you doing this for a living?"

A flush of colour stained her cheeks, as she stared at him in genuine surprise. *Ha*, he finally had the upper hand in this bizarre encounter.

"I... I'm going to do a degree in music. I need to build up a nest egg so I can study full time," she said.

"Great plan."

"I thought so."

Dev leaned against the doorjamb. "By all means, please continue. Do I get to choose another song? Sixties jaunty pop hits were never my thing."

"That's not how the system works."

"It *is* my birthday. Don't I get to bend a few rules?"

"Which song did you have in mind?"

"'What's new Pussycat?'"

"Very funny." The acerbic tone had returned.

"What about 'Memory'."

"From the *Cats* movie?"

"Personally, I prefer to link the song to the original stage production, but I'll leave the artistic choice to you."

"Either way, not gonna happen."

Dev rolled his eyes in mock resignation. “Fine, jaunty sixties pop tune it is, then.”

This time he didn’t interrupt. Instead, he concentrated on the crystal-clear quality of her voice. Yes, she was inexperienced, and her breathing technique needed work, but the raw ability underneath that lack of training was incredible.

She bobbed a quick curtsey when she’d finished, pulling a burst of laughter from him, which turned into a wince as his hangover complained. “I’m in desperate need of coffee. Would you like to come in and join me?”

“Sorry, that’s against the rules.”

“Is it against the rules to ask your name?”

“Kat.”

“That *was* a genuine question.”

“It’s a genuine answer. Kat with a K, short for Katherine.” Damn, the dancing mischief in her eyes was addictive, as were her quicksilver mood changes.

“I’m running late. Happy birthday.” With a jaunty wave, she turned to go.

Dev racked his brain for a way of delaying her departure, and came up empty. “Katherine.”

She paused with her hand on the door of a small yellow sedan.

"Good luck with the degree."

She lifted one shoulder in a self-conscious shrug. "I need to be accepted first. The school I've applied to is *really* exclusive."

"Which school?"

"One you've probably never heard of. A private college called Perdies in Claremont." She slid behind the wheel and within seconds was gone, leaving him staring at an empty parking space.

Yes, he'd heard of Perdies College of Music.

After all, he owned it.

Minutes later Dev was on the phone to his PA.

"How's the hangover, boss?" she asked.

"Terrible. Jules, has the admissions shortlist been finalised for next semester?"

"Not yet. The committee are compiling it now."

"Can you courier all the applications to me here at home?"

"*All* of them? There are hundreds. I thought you'd planned a relaxing, work-free zone birthday."

"I've changed my mind."

Kat shoved the lurid blue, tiny peaked cap back from her forehead. It immediately fell forward over her eyes. No matter how many bobby pins she jammed into the stupid thing, it refused to stay put. While she was in full adjustment mode, she yanked at the matching dress's short skirt, which pulled the neckline downwards, displaying an alarming amount of cleavage.

Dammit, every time she tugged at some part of this Sexy Stewardess, or Flirty Flight Attendant...or whatever they called this *ridiculous* costume, something else popped out, or rode upwards. The size label declared it to be a twelve. *No way is this a twelve*. And there was no way she could win this tug of war. Turning to peer out of the window, she watched for her taxi. A flat car battery had already cost her a shift at the university cafe this morning. She refused to lose an entire day's pay today, even if her profits were diminished by a cab fare. She ran 'Come Fly With Me' through her mind a couple more times, committing the song lyrics to memory. Hopefully, the retiring commercial pilot would appreciate her professional dedication, or else he'd assume she was a stripagram and try to pinch her bum.

After another quick check for wardrobe malfunctions, Kat grabbed her bag and made her way downstairs, taking care not to trip on the high stilettos. The postman was just leaving, so she checked her mail. The result was two takeaway menus and an electricity bill. *Wonderful.*

The dull ping of the lift, and the squeak of a rubber tipped cane on tiles, made her turn with a smile. "Mrs. Jenkins, you're home. How was the cruise?"

Her neighbour's broad grin said it all. "Wonderful, my dear. Fourteen days of being waited on hand and foot and watching the ocean go by without a care in the world. I even won the bingo jackpot two days in a row." She unlocked her post box and pulled a stack of paper from it. Catalogues and junk mail fluttered to the floor.

Kat stooped to pick them up. "You could have asked me to check your mail while you were away."

"It's fine, Katherine. I don't get a lot these days anyway."

Katherine. No one used her full name, apart from her lovely neighbour, and a certain tall, dark, rumpled, gorgeously dishevelled mess of a feline loving client from a few weeks back.

"I took lots of holiday photos if you'd like to see them." Mrs. Jenkins cut into her visual memories.

"I'd love to." A sharp toot of a horn announced the taxi's arrival. "I'll pop in for tea later this afternoon if you like."

"That would be lovely... oh, wait, this letter's addressed to you. I swear that new postman's dyslectic, he's always mixing up his numbers," she held out a white envelope.

"Thanks." Kat took it from her and shoved it in her bag as the impatient taxi driver gave the horn another blast.

Her smooth progress to the upscale city pub lasted exactly five minutes before they hit snail pace traffic. Flashing blue lights up ahead made the reason obvious. "Can we go another way?" she asked.

The driver's answer was a non-verbal and unhelpful grunt. Today was *not* her day. Her phone beeped with a message.

Pilot sick, gig cancelled.

"What?" Kat glared at it, and slumped back in her seat. Damn, this *really* was not her day. "Change of plans, can you take me home, please?"

"Hope you're not in a hurry."

"Unfortunately, not." She shoved the phone back in her bag. The stiff white envelope brushed her fingers, and having nothing else to occupy her time, Kat pulled it out.

For a full five seconds, she stared at the gold embossed lettering in the left-hand corner. *Perdies College of Music.*

Her tummy did a flip flop. It was a rejection letter, it had to be. Despite pouring over the application form for hours, and chewing her way through three pen caps, many of the questions relating to 'professional experience' had been left painfully blank. Sure, she could have listed her singing telegram assignments, but foolish pride had stopped her. The result had looked amateurish. Hope had kept her checking the post every day for a few weeks, then she'd all but given up. No doubt the rejection would be coined in the most professional and polite terms. Something like, *Dear Miss Grant. Thank you for your application. We regret to inform you...*

With as much enthusiasm as ripping a band aid off a wound, Kat slid her finger along the envelope's edge and pulled out the single sheet of embossed paper.

Dear Miss Grant. Thank you for your application. An interview has been set up for you at 1pm on...

A rush of adrenalin sent a jolt through her body. Kat read the date once, twice, three times. No. That couldn't be right, it *couldn't* be.

"Excuse me," she tapped the driver on the shoulder. "What's today's date?"

He gave her a raised brow look in the rear-view mirror. "The 16th."

She knew that. She'd checked her emails this morning. She'd read the paper. She'd watched the morning news. Of course, it was the 16th. This was ridiculous, impossible. Why would Perdies arrange an interview on such short notice—

The answer struck with sickening clarity. Turning over the envelope, she peered at the postmark. The letter was mailed the day Mrs. Jenkins left on her cruise. Kat had been checking her own mailbox daily, and all this time the letter that could change her life was sitting, unread, mere feet away.

1pm

The next stomach-turning jolt came hot on the heels of the first. “Excuse me, what’s the time?”

“Almost noon.”

Sucking in deep breaths, Kat dragged a hand through her hair, dislodging the silly little hat and half a dozen bobby pins. “I need to get to Claremont.”

The driver stopped his perusal of road ahead and half turned in his seat. “Sorry?”

“Change of plan, again. I need to get to Claremont right now.”

He gestured to the non-moving traffic surrounding them. “We’re not going anywhere right now.”

Kat fought the restricting seatbelt to peer out the window. “The other side’s clear. Can’t you do a quick U-turn?”

“What?”

“Look, this is important.”

“So is my taxi license.”

Another taxi pulled into a restaurant across the street. Kat made a snap decision. “Thanks. I’m getting out here.” she shoved a twenty in his general direction and dove out the door, ignoring his disgruntled complaints. Her ankle turned as she dodged traffic and raced across the road. Kat ignored the pain and snagged the other taxi just before he pulled away.

"Claremont, please." She rattled off the full address at high speed and collapsed into another worn leather seat, praying for clear roads.

Smoothing out the crumpled letter still in her hand, Kat read the full content. *Please bring your full resume.* Nope, that wouldn't happen. *Please bring along sheet music for your performance.* Okay, this was getting worse by the second.

She tugged down the snug skirt riding high on her thighs. She was going for an interview with the most prestigious music school in the state, completely unprepared, and dressed as a sexy stewardess. Oh yeah, this was all going *so* well.

The butterflies in her stomach morphed into a swarm of bees as the taxi pulled up outside the historic three storey building in its beautiful tree lined street at precisely twelve fifty-five pm. "Thank you," she handed over the fare with a generous tip, and stood by the entrance.

A brass intercom beckoned. Clearing her throat, Kat pressed it. "I'm here for an appointment?"

The door clicked open, revealing a long marble floored corridor with a desk at the end. Kat's stiletto heels rang on the hard surface like a tolling bell of doom.

"Hi. Katherine Grant, is it? Please take a seat." The receptionist's cheery yellow designer dress and sunny smile were in complete contrast to the traditional décor surrounding her.

Kat lowered herself into one of the rich leather chairs lining the corridor. The opening line to Memory, sung in a nervous sounding soprano voice, drifted to her from a closed door to her right.

"Can I choose another song? What about Memory."

Kat welcomed the mental flashback for what it was, a distraction to sooth her jangling nerves. She let her mind wander; recalling every gorgeous inch of luscious, rumpled virility, from the top of his curly, sleep mussed hair, to the bare feet peeking out from below well-worn track pants. He'd been a veritable smorgasbord of eye candy, even with black ink scrawled across his forehead.

No one has the right to look that good with a hangover.

Her musings on Mr. Deliciously Dishevelled were interrupted for the second time that day when the receptionist made an odd sound, somewhere between a groan and a sigh. Kat threw her an enquiring look.

"Sorry. We're all sick of hearing that song," she said.

"I thought everyone loved 'Memory'?"

"Trust me, it loses its appeal after the first few thousand renditions, and just when it slipped off the radar, they make a damn *movie* and we get bombarded again."

"Thanks for the tip."

A door to her left, bearing a brass number 3, opened to reveal a tall, slender woman dressed impeccably in a black trouser suit. She shook the hand of someone inside and strode out of the building without a backward glance, radiating confidence in every step.

"You're welcome." The receptionist called after her, giving Kat a sideways wink and a grin. "Artists." Her tone dripped with disdain.

"Do you ever wonder if you're working in the wrong place?" Kat asked, with an answering smile.

"*All* the time." Her laughter was rich and honest, and contagious. Kat had to bite her tongue before renewed nerves got the better of her and create a giggle fit she'd be powerless to control.

Her friendly ally glanced at the pad in front of her. "Room 3, Miss Grant," she paused and touched her earpiece. "Sorry? Really? Oh, okay. Make that Room 1, Miss Grant. You're seeing Mr. Perdie first."

"The... the owner?"

"Yep, that's him, my boss. Room 1, straight ahead. Good luck."

Sucking in a lungful of air, Kat pushed open the solid wooden door, and stopped dead in her tracks.

"Good afternoon, Katherine. Interesting costume. Let me guess, flirty flight attendant?"

The deliciously dishevelled look had vanished, replaced by a crisp white shirt topped with a black suit jacket. His dark hair was smooth instead of sleep mussed, but the devilish smile remained.

Perdies... Purr as in cat. *Oh God.*

Kat spun on her heel and walked out.

"Katherine? Katherine? Wait up, where are you going?"

She kept walking, past the surprised looking receptionist, along the never-ending corridor "I didn't know."

"Know what?" his voice was close behind her.

"First the leotard, now this stupid outfit. This wasn't how I imagined this. I look ridiculous. What must you think of me?" Kat yanked open the heavy front door.

"To be honest, I'm wondering how on earth you're walking so fast in those shoes."

Kat scanned the streets, *please let there be another taxi*. She dragged her hands through her hair in agitation and kept walking.

"Umm, Katherine, regarding your outfit, reconsider putting your arms up like that. The jogger across the street just ran into a tree."

With cheeks blazing, Kat yanked down the treacherous hemline, all without looking back or breaking stride.

"Will you please stop?" he caught her arm, halting her forward momentum.

Left with no alternative, she turned to face him, holding her chin high, despite the heated blush still burning her cheeks. "I didn't know you were you."

"Okay, I think."

"You're supposed to be D. Jones not Devlin Perdie."

"Keep going, I'm marginally less confused."

"That's what it said on that singing telegram booking. D. Jones. You'll think I planned this, *all* of this, some stupid amateur trying to get your attention and get into your posh school, but I didn't. The agency gave me the assignment." Kat heard her voice rise in pitch and tried to step away.

Instead of releasing her, his fingers slid along her arm to enclose her fingers. "It's a natural assumption, about the name. It has nothing to do with my love of cats, if that's what you're implying. Perdie is Mums maiden name. I named the school to honour her love of music."

"Oh."

"My legal name is D. Jones, Devlin Sebastian Jones if you want the full version. I go by Perdie for business purposes. The pseudonym helps maintain my privacy. No, I didn't think you planned any of this."

"Why?"

"Call it instinct? Even if you had contrived some convoluted plot, it wouldn't have worked. I don't respond well to stunts. Last year, a woman tracked down my private number and sent a video of herself performing Waltzing Matilda in the nude. It did *not* result in an interview at my college."

His hand was warm, wrapped around hers. Rough calluses on the pads of his fingers teased her skin. A vision popped into her head of him strumming a Spanish guitar, with sleep mussed hair and morning stubble. Kat shoved away the intriguing image.

Devlin Perdie, or Jones, was still talking. "Let's tackle some of your other questions. No, you don't look ridiculous. Yes, your outfit is *way* too small."

Kat yanked her fingers free of his to give the skirt a final pointless yank. "You mean to tell me all of this, me being here, is all a weird coincidence?"

"Ah, in the interest of full disclosure, after our unorthodox initial meeting I did read your application and added you to the shortlist."

Another emotion, a deep-seated resentment of handouts, rose inside Kat, bringing with it a bitter taste of disappointment. She turned her back on him, determined to find a taxi.

"Hold on. *Now,* where are you going?"

"I'm not a charity case."

"Who said you were?"

"I filled in that application. I know how pathetic it looked."

"Will you slow down? Jesus, are those heels motorised?"

"I wanted to achieve this on my merit."

"You did, Katherine." He grabbed her hand a second time before she'd gotten half way down the street. "Good God, I should have guessed you'd be this stubborn. Come back with me and I'll prove it to you." Without waiting for an answer, he began walking in the opposite direction.

"I'm coming. You can let go."

"Given your tendency to take off at a moment's notice, I don't think so. Are you training for the Olympic sprint team in your spare time?"

"Exercise is good for lung capacity. It helps my singing."

"See? You do deserve the interview."

Kat ignored the teasing air in his voice. As they re-entered Perdies, the receptionist glanced at their clasped hands, her stare openly curious.

"Katherine, meet Jules, my PA who doubles as receptionist during interviews. Jules, can you bring

Katherine's application in to my office, please?" Devlin said.

Instead of taking his place behind the desk, as she expected, he remained standing, although he did finally release her hand, which she was absolutely, positively *not* disappointed about.

"I read all the applications for this semester. Do you know why yours stood out? Everyone else sent YouTube links, or Instagram posts of various performances. One applicant even arranged a mini concert complete with professional lighting and staging."

"I'm not on social media."

"Good. Perdies is about music, not being the latest online celebrity." He broke off when Jules walked into his office and handed him a manila folder. He pulled a flash drive from inside. "You sent this, Katherine. An audio recording. No video, no music, no gimmicks, just a voice. That simple act set you apart from countless other candidates. You're worried about your lack of professional experience? It means nothing to us. Our aim is to train singers who have natural talent, not to guarantee stardom. My acquisitions team pick students who have the determination to work hard and learn." His lips kicked up in a mischievous smile, "I think we've already established your determined nature." Handing her the folder, he walked to his desk and leaned against it, hands shoved into his pants pockets, looking every inch the smart, urban, unreasonably handsome, businessman. "What do you say? Did I pass *my* Perdies interview?"

"I have a few questions."

"I expected nothing less."

"Does your Mum sing?"

One dark winged brow rose at the change of subject. "Every day. She inspires me."

"Do you always read every application?"

"I try to. I want to. We're receiving more and more every semester and sometimes the workload gets on top of me. I trust my acquisitions team to select the right applicants when I can't. You should know one more thing. The admissions committee, which doesn't include me, decide final placements after the probation period ends."

"Good."

"I thought you'd approve. No special treatment, Katherine, you have my word."

"Do you always see the applicants before their interviews?"

His hesitation rendered the answer unnecessary. "Promise you won't bolt? I heard you talking to Jules, and wanted to see the look on your face when you saw it was me."

Kat folded her arms across her chest. "I see."

He pushed away from the desk, to stand mere inches from her, his voice lowered to a sexy enticement. "Come on, would you really deny me my ta-da moment?"

"I have a question."

"*Another* question, you mean?" Pure mischief danced in those sexy green eyes.

"Did you watch the whole naked Waltzing Matilda video?"

"Of course not. She had a terrible voice."

The horror in his tone pulled a reluctant laugh from her. "Last question."

"Fire away."

"How long did it take to get that writing off your forehead?"

"A week. I swear I scrubbed so much, it left a scar."

They both laughed, the shared moment of intimacy easing the tension. The trouble was, Perdies owner looked *way* too good when he laughed. For the sake of her professionalism Kat put some distance between them, but paused by his office door. "I'm going to my actual interview now, even though I look ludicrous."

"I like the outfit. Does it have a hat? I feel it needs a hat."

"I left it in the taxi."

"Shame."

"This is crazy. I don't have my resume, or any sheet music on me."

"I already know you can sing in live performance. Tell Bill he can skip that part."

"You just said *no* special treatment." Kat fixed him with a glare.

Devlin threw up his hands in defeat. "Fine. I'm sure Jules has music you can use. Go through to Room 3 when you're ready."

"Thank you. And thank you for this opportunity, Mr. *Perdie*."

His warm chuckle followed her when she closed the door behind her with a firm click.

Chapter Two

Considering the slap stick comedy antics of her initial Perdies involvement, the actual acceptance of her probation went smoothly. Less than one week after her interview, she received a letter in the mail, signed D. Perdie in a sweeping hand. With some justifiable pride, she held it out to her boss at the university café. “The classes include most mornings, and some full days. Which means I might fit in a few shifts here and there, as long as I don’t get too much homework—” Her words were cut off by one of Gino’s famous Italian bear hugs, removing all oxygen from her lungs.

"We are so proud of you. Soon you will have no need of me and my small café. You will be too famous. I shall tell everyone I knew you at the start."

She laughed, trying to untangle herself from his enthusiasm before she suffocated. "Let's not get carried away. This is just eight weeks probation. Only five out of fifteen applicants go on from here."

"You will be one of these five, I am sure of it. As for the extra shifts? You will be welcome anytime. All of my customers love you."

Kat swallowed the lump in her throat. Gino knew she needed to earn her way in the world, and he respected her for it. He was the closest thing she had to a father now, and she adored him. "Thank you. I'll get my official class schedule today and email it."

"Speaking of customers, be sure to see the twins before you go, they have been asking for you." He jerked his head to the coffee counter where two of her favourite regulars were trying to peer into the kitchen area.

"Well?"

"Did you get in?"

"Tell us you got in."

"C'mon, Kat, don't leave us hanging."

John and Jason weren't just twins; they were identical and had the tendency to finish each other's thoughts. The one-sentence-per-twin style of conversation was challenging, until you got used to their unique synchronicity.

She held out the letter. "I'm in."

Their whoops and over the top high fives drew more than a few curious stares from the other customers.

"I knew it," Jason said.

"No way. I knew it first." his brother scowled at him.

"Whatever. We're both stoked for you."

Apart from Gino, the twins were the only ones who knew about her life, her difficult teenage years, and her love of singing. She'd confided in them one afternoon when business was slow and she needed someone to talk to. "Thanks. Your support means a lot."

"We'll still see you, right?"

"You're not deserting us?"

"Would I do that?" She wagged a finger at them. "Besides, even if I didn't come back for five years, you two would still be here." Jason and John were perpetual students. As far as she could work out, at the ripe old age of nineteen, they were somehow studying for their second degree. She was only six years older than them, but their lives were polar opposite. Kat glanced at the clock on the café wall. “Listen, can we chat another time? My first class is this afternoon and I don’t want to be late.”

“Sure.”

“Will do.”

“Break an arm.”

John threw his brother a dramatic eye roll. “It’s break a leg, moron.”

“How would I know that? What does it even mean?”

“Who knows? It’s just something people say.”

Kat chuckled, and gave up trying to interrupt the back-and-forth flow. She left them, still arguing, said a final goodbye to Gino and a few regular customers, and drove to Claremont, giving herself heaps of extra time in case of unforeseen hassles. There were none and she arrived at Perdies with an hour to spare.

Because of her two previous fashion faux pas, she’d gone through her entire wardrobe before settling on jeans, ballet flats and her favourite red sweater. The very first person she saw when she made her way down the entrance corridor was Devlin. He looked up from his conversation with Jules, and gave her a thorough, sweeping perusal from her head to her toes and back again, ending with a teasing half smile and a thumbs up sign.

Kat wasn't sure if she should laugh, or hit him.

"Hi," someone stepped into eyeline, blocking her view of Perdie's owner. "Are you a newbie too?"

"Yep." Her enthusiastic fellow probationary student was easy on the eye. Dark hair, cut in a jagged style fell across one eye, giving him a trendy, lopsided look, which fitted with the multi-coloured shirt and skin tight jeans. He couldn't have been more than twenty and the passion and excitement in his eyes was clear to see.

"Are you a singer?" she asked him.

"Flautist." He raised the slender leather box in his hand. "I'm Tom. Ava's just coming. She's a newbie too, we met at our interview. Guess what she plays?"

The answer was self-evident as the tiny Japanese woman struggled through the main door, dragging a cello case with her. "A bit of help would be good." She threw Tom a scathing look.

Kat dove for the door before it closed in her face. "I'm beginning to see an advantage of being a singer."

Tom was chuckling as he wrangled the enormous case into the hallway. "I already told her, pick a smaller instrument, for heaven's sake."

"You know what they say about men who go small... they do it for a reason." Ava's eyes dropped to his groin, the mischief on her face belaying the innocence of her angelic features.

Kat bit back a strangled laugh as other artists spilled though the door, some carrying instruments, some carrying sheet music. Soon the hallway filled with people, and echoed with enthusiastic, nervous voices. The excitement in the air was palpable. Never had Kat felt so *in tune* with the people around her. When Jules cleared her throat, it cut through the wall of noise. Everyone turned to her in unison.

"Newbies, get your asses into the meeting room to your left. Please leave your instruments outside, I promise no one will steal them. Mr. Perdie will join you shortly."

Hearing the owners name sent an extra frisson of excitement through the entire group. They shuffled in, jostling for position. Kat hung back, happy to sit at the back. To her surprise, the two musicians joined her.

"Do you think he'll have it with him?" Ava asked.

"He's bound to. It's tradition."

Kat glanced between them in confusion. "Have what?"

"The cane. The famous cane," this from Tom.

Ava craned her neck to see into the hallway. "I've read rumours online that it's some sort of muscular disease, or a deformity, you know, like Phantom of the Opera."

Muscular disease? Deformity? Kat flashed back to Devlin chasing her down the street. If there was any sort of movement problem, he had shown no sign of it. "Where are you getting this stuff? Devlin Jo–Perdie doesn't have a social media profile, does he?"

Ava grinned at her obvious lack of knowledge. "That's the point. He keeps everything personal totally private. It's *all* about the school. Why do you think everyone's so interested? The online forums are always talking about him. No one even knows where he lives."

I do. Kat bit her lip to keep from smiling.

The sharp rap of metal hitting solid wood reverberated around them, rendering the room to pin-drop silence in an instant. Devlin strode in, with an ornately carved dark wood cane in one hand. He tapped it as he walked, the sound in perfect rhythm to his footsteps. All the students followed his progress across the room, their heads moving in a slow turn, like the open-mouthed clowns in a sideshow alley game. *Nice entrance, Mr. Jones.*

"Good morning, everyone, and welcome to Perdies. May I congratulate you on getting this far. Our criteria selection gets more and more difficult each semester." He leaned against the mantle of an old fireplace, with both hands clasped around the silver head of the cane. "The first thing I'd like you to learn today is about the music that surrounds you. Can you hear it?" he scanned the crowds. Kat resisted the urge to duck to avoid his gaze. Not that he'd pay any attention to her, or single her out. She was just a student now, the same as everyone else.

"Music exists in every aspect of your lives. In the wind blowing through the trees, in the patter of rain on a tin roof, even in the sound of your own heart. It sounds cliché, but it's true." He tapped the cane on the floor in a steady rhythmic beat, and kept it up while he spoke. Tap, *tap*, tap *tap*. Kat's own heartbeat began a sympathetic resonance. "The sooner you accept and embrace this world of music, the sooner you'll incorporate it into your own life, into your own talent. Perdies can't teach you how to be a musician, or a singer, and we won't try. What we will do over the next eight weeks is help you unlock the music in your soul, and hopefully set it free." Tap, *tap*, tap, *tap*. A bomb could have gone off in that room, and no one would have moved. Kat wasn't sure if her fellow students were even breathing, the silence was so absolute, apart from the continuous echo of a silver and wooden heart.

This was their dream, their passion, perfectly encapsulated in a few simple words and a subtle, but powerful demonstration.

It's my dream too.

Kat sent a silent thank you to the man at the front of the class who'd made it happen.

When the rhythmic sound stopped, everyone around her drew a collective breath. "And, remember, you're here to have fun too." Devlin grinned, breaking the intensity of the moment and replacing it with genuine laughter from his captivated students. "I will hand you over to some of your teachers, who'll go through the schedule for the probationary period and answer all your questions. Once again, I'd like to welcome you all here. Perdies exists because of you." He pushed away from the mantle, as a grey-haired man took centre stage and fiddled with the papers in his hands.

Ava leaned across her to whisper "God, he can pluck my strings anytime."

Tom let out a heartfelt sigh. "Not before he blows my... instrument."

Ava's snort was unladylike. "You're dreaming if you think he's gay."

"Why? You don't know for sure he's straight. It's not like we have our likes and dislikes written across our forehead."

Devlin had.

Kat, who'd been fighting to contain her laughter, failed in the attempt and covered the strangled giggle with a cough. She thumped her chest a couple of times for authenticity when they gave her curious looks.

Her attention was torn between the banter of her new found friends, and Devlin. Instead of leaving via the door he'd entered, he was walking along the length of the room, past the rows of seats. When he caught her gaze and held it, her heart skipped a beat.

Don't, don't you dare, don't you dare.

"Katherine." He inclined his head and kept walking, exiting through a door at the back.

Tom and Ava stopped talking to stare at her, as did numerous other students who swivelled in their chairs.

Kat waved her hand, aiming for nonchalance and pushing the heat from her cheeks through sheer force of will. "I met him during my preliminary interview. Pretty embarrassing, as I had no idea who he was." *Truer words were never spoken.*

"He's hot." A female student rested her chin on the back of her chair with a dreamy expression. "Do you think we'll see much of him?"

"I hope so," someone answered from a few rows further forward.

"What do you think he looks like first thing in the morning?" the breathy question came from yet another star struck female.

Deliciously dishevelled.

Kat kept that piece of information firmly under wraps, though.

The succinct clearing of a throat had them sitting up straighter and turning to the front of the room, like naughty ten-year olds caught chatting in class.

"I hope you all have paper and pens, we have a lot to get through."

People scrambled for writing implements, and the probationary semester at Perdies officially began.

The rest of the day passed in a blur. She chatted to other students, both old and new, surprised how keen the more experienced musicians were to talk. No one looked down on the newbies, not once did she consider herself inferior to those who'd been studying under Perdies regime for one, two or even three years. An open classroom policy meant people were welcome to sit in on lectures and lessons even if they didn't relate to their particular expertise. Kat jumped at the chance, and threw herself headfirst into the frenetic class schedule. She learnt about violins, guitars, and thoroughly enjoyed the cellist class, waving at Ava when she was asked to perform in front of everyone. Kat knew even if she never made it past the probation period, the sheer amount of knowledge she'd gain in these next few weeks would be invaluable.

She took copious notes, filling up one entire notebook, and had to dash out during a tea break to buy a second one, plus a stack of pens and pencils. The only pencil case she could find at short notice to store her hoard was a *Hello Kitty* one, and she shoved it in her bag, hoping Devlin wouldn't catch a glimpse.

Speaking of Perdies owner, she saw him only in occasional glimpses too—not that she was searching him out— He had an interesting tendency to lean on things. Sometimes with his shoulder on a doorjamb standing with arms crossed over his chest. Sometimes with his hip resting on the corner of a desk as he talked to Jules or other Perdies staff members. One moment stayed with her, late in the afternoon, when she caught him standing with arms folded staring out of a window, as if something were weighing on his mind. It was a momentary blip on his gregarious landscape as he seemed keen to share his day with as many employees as possible.

His favourite position was with his back against a wall and his hands on the head of the cane. One thing was obvious. He exuded a casual, effortless almost languorous grace in whatever he did, *like a cat*.

Kat gave herself a mental slap, and focussed on the teacher discussing breathing techniques for singing opera.

People drifted off when the last class of the day was over. A few stragglers remained behind, taking notes, or rehearsing. Kat lingered to the last, unwilling to let this special day end. Her teachers had taken pity on the newbies, letting them off with a homework free night. With nothing else to occupy her time, Kat explored. Some of the offices on the ground floor, like Devlin's, had *"Staff Only"* signs on them. All the other rooms seemed fair game. She peeked into several, finding a few rooms housing beautiful pianos, some obvious meeting rooms like the one they'd gathered in that morning, and various other spaces set up for general purpose. She explored the lower levels until good manners won over pure curiosity. The last thing she wanted on her first day was to be scolded for nosiness. Intending to have just a quick look upstairs, she found the library tucked away on the third floor, a paradise of a room, jam packed with books from floor to ceiling. Within minutes she was sitting barefoot on the floor, lost in a dog-eared biography of Edith Piaf.

"You can leave, you know. We don't keep our student's prisoners."

Kat let out a startled squeak and looked up to see Devlin leaning against the doorjamb.

"I don't want to leave. I've died and gone to heaven."

The teasing half smile made an appearance. "Please don't die on your first day. It ruins my stats. Tell me you at least ate something and didn't just bounce from class to class all day."

She nodded her agreement. "I brought sandwiches from home, and Ava shared her sushi with me."

"Ava? Ah, yeah. Cellist, probationary, right?"

"You know all your students?"

"I try to."

From somewhere below her came the soft cry of a French horn. From a different direction in the building she heard singing, a clear male tenor. "How on earth do you get anything done around here? I feel like I'm surrounded by music. It's like I've come home." The frank admission caused the heat of a blush to scald her cheeks. Kat ducked her head, fiddling with the pages of the paperback.

Devlin dropped to an easy crouch, balancing on the balls of his feet, bringing him to eye level. "There are days when I get nothing done. Sometimes I close my eyes and just listen."

He understood. No one had ever understood her obsession of music. Kat shook off the emotional pull, tugging her ever closer into his charismatic orbit. She gestured to his half-seated position. "Should you be doing that? Without the aid of your walking stick?"

To her surprise, a look of embarrassment crossed his handsome features. "The cane. There is a story behind that."

"I guessed there would be."

"A few years ago, I strained my knee while I was out jogging. It was the day before the newbies started. The bloody thing was killing me, but I came in anyway. It only took an hour of climbing up and down these stairs before I knew I needed to find some sort of crutch, or go home."

"You scouted out the local antique shops in absolute agony and bought an elaborate, silver tipped cane? Most people would have popped to the nearest chemist."

He grinned at her teasing. "I *found* the cane right here, in one of the upstairs rooms, hidden in a cupboard."

"You're kidding."

"I swear it's the truth. The students seemed to like it, and, it started a trend on social media. I figured as long as the online community were focussing on my cane, instead of my personal life, I may as well keep using it. And, it has a secondary purpose. It makes a great metronome," he tapped his fingers on the wooden floor boards in the same tempo he'd used that morning. Her eyes were drawn to that small rhythmic movement.

"Your privacy is important to you. I know more about you than the others. Weren't you worried I'd gossip?"

"Not for a moment. I trust you, Katherine."

Damn, he had to stop saying things like that. She peered around the room, needing a different focus. "You've created something special here for your students, a haven."

"Thank you." He snagged a book from one of the lower shelves. "If you like bios, read this one. Caruso had a fascinating life. This one is excellent if you want technical know-how, or these two." He added more and more books from the pile, plucking them from various places with familiar ease. Mimicking her cross-legged position on the floor, he launched into a description of the merits of each and every one. The passion was clear in his voice, but Kat barely heard. His knee was almost touching hers. His citrus aftershave created a subtle tingle along her nerve endings. At least, she assumed it was the aftershave. He'd smelt gorgeous on his doorstep, with pre shave stubble. Maybe it was his cologne. Moisturiser? Hair product?

For heaven's sake, stop thinking about how good he smells.

"You've read all of these?" Kat pulled her mind back to the business at hand.

"More than once."

"Thanks for the recommendations, but there are only so many books I can get through in eight weeks."

"No rush. You can keep them as long as you like."

"Eight weeks is the probation period. It's part of *your* rules, remember?"

"I can see you being here for a lot longer than that—wait, don't hit me. I'm referring purely to your talent."

Kat lowered the book she'd threatened him with. "Fine, I'll read the Caruso first and see how I go."

He rose to his feet with that fluid grace, holding out his hand. "Come on, Miss Grant, it's getting late. I'll walk you to your car. You need to go home and eat dinner if you're to keep up this brutal class hopping pace."

"Were you spying on me?"

"Observing you. Completely different thing."

Okay, there wasn't a suitable reply to that statement, none she could think of, anyway. "Everything here is beautiful." Kat ran her hands along the jarrah railing on their descent down the stairs.

"It is indeed." The look he gave her was warm, in a head spinning, sexy sort of way.

"Be careful. Looks like the security lights have blown. It's dark out here," he pushed open the rear door, heading into the parking area. "Where's your car?"

Kat was surprised to see the sun had well and truly set. How long had they been talking? "Over there, by the fence. You can go inside. I'll be fine."

"I don't want you falling."

"You've seen me run in heels."

"Fair point, I—" his voice dropped away.

"Devlin? *Devlin?* Where'd you go?" Kat felt around beside her in the dark and came up with empty air.

"Ouch, down here. I tripped over the ornamental rockery."

"What? Are you hurt?" She dropped to her knees, searching for him, her questing hands encountering the fine wool of his trousers. His quick intake of breath was her first clue, even before her fingers brushed against the zipper at his groin. Kat yanked her hand away. Great, now she was *groping* him.

"Is my chin bleeding?"

"I can't see. Stay there, let me get my phone." Kat rummaged through her shoulder bag, and flicked on the phone's torch app. Light flooded the area, revealing Perdies owner sprawled on the ground, one foot snagged under a large rock.

"I knew that bloody rockery was a bad idea." He dabbed the grazes on his chin and cheek.

"Here," she handed him a tissue. "Can you move? Is anything broken?"

"Only my ego."

All that languid grace and elegance had vanished, lost in an awkward tangle of limbs. Kat bit her lip to fight off a giggle.

"Are you laughing, Katherine?"

"No." The single, high-pitched word would have made a castrato envious.

"I think you're lying."

Kat tried, and failed, to claw back control, finally conceding to laughter even as she waved her hands in apology, sending the torch beam bouncing around them. "I'm sorry. I'm so sorry."

"Don't be. That sound is well worth the loss of my blood, and my pride." Amusement coloured his words.

Another student, it sounded like Tom, called out from the back door. "Hello? Is everything alright out here?"

"Call the landscaper, tell him he's fired." Devlin said from the floor, sending Kat into a secondary giggle fit.

"Miss Grant, if you can stop laughing long enough, I need you to do something for me."

"What?"

"Go back inside and get that bloody cane."

Chapter Three

Dev added a dollop of honey to the mug, and inhaled the aromatic steam. His timing was perfect, as the latest group session spilled out of the classroom one floor above, their voices and laughter reaching him before their actual presence.

Within seconds, the kitchen area was swamped. Most headed for the high-tech coffee machine, some raided cupboards for their preferred variety of tea. He stood to one side, answering the chorus of greetings, letting the students indulge their caffeine needs.

A few people stared at the sticking plaster on his chin, and he saw more than a few hidden smiles.

News of his nocturnal tumble in the garden had no doubt spread. It didn't matter. One person in particular was on his mind, and she was nowhere to be seen. He'd all but given up hope before she appeared, lingering on the stairway, her hand on the rail, her face turned to the side. Dev was tempted to grab his phone and snap a picture, capturing her in a moment of quiet contemplation amid the human chatter and clinking of spoons against china. He resisted the urge, Katherine's privacy was as important to her as his was. The freshly hydrated crowd scattered to the four corners, leaving him alone with a rich fragrant mixture of coffee beans and herbal teas.

"Ouch. Does that hurt?" Katherine descended the last stair to stand by his side.

"Only when I laugh."

"How's the foot? I should have stayed last night and helped."

"Don't worry. I had the indignity of calling my mother to come to the school and drive me home *and* to the doctors this morning. I've wrenched my ankle, that's all. It'll be fine in a day or two."

"I feel like it was my fault."

"It wasn't. I'm glad it was me and not you, and anyway I have my cane." Dev grinned, because Katherine's attention was clearly not on him. "Actually, I'm in excruciating agony and need all the sympathy I can get."

He was rewarded by the flush of pink across her cheeks. She tilted her head towards the stairwell, her distraction obvious. "I'm sorry, I'm just trying to listen to something. Can you hear that piano? It's incredible."

He tuned out the voices around him and dialled his senses into instrumental only, a trick easily accomplished after years of practice. "Anna was our top probation student last year. In her final performance exam, she played Moonlight Sonata and had all the committee in tears."

"I'm not surprised. I wish I could hear it better. My first instinct was to go and eavesdrop by the door."

"I have a better idea. Follow me. You've already discovered the library, let me show you another one of Perdies' secrets." He led them to a small music room on the first level, tucked away at the back. "Not many people use this room, it has the nickname of 'the sunroom' for obvious reasons. It gets the afternoon sun, and most students find it too warm. But, if you open the window, you'll discover why it's one of my favourites." Katherine swung open one of the lead light panes. Piano music filled the small space, filtering down from the third floor.

The look on her face brought a smile to his. "It's a sweet spot for the floors above. Don't ask me why."

"And it comes with a window seat, how wonderful." She sat down on the wide ledge, tucking one jean clad leg under her. "Why can I smell liquorice?"

"It's the tea. I made it for you." He handed over the mug.

"Why?"

The question made him chuckle. "To soothe your throat."

"My throat is fine."

Dev looked to heaven for guidance. "It's a singers blend, something Mum created years ago. Joan, one of the third years was complaining of a strained throat, so I made her a pot. I poured the extra into a mug for you, because your class was about to end. Drink the damn tea, Katherine."

She cradled the floral-patterned mug in her hands with a murmured thank you.

"You're welcome. I'll give you the recipe."

"I don't like—"

"Special treatment, yes, I'm very aware." Dev sat opposite her on the window seat. "I spend way too much time in this room. For some reason my presence makes the students nervous. They stuff up when I'm watching them. A problem you've never experienced."

That stubborn chin of hers headed skyward, although for once she didn't verbally respond to his teasing. He joined her in silence, listening to the emotive strains of Liebestraum.

As the next piece of music began, a more upbeat Mozart sonata, Katherine ran her fingers along the painted window frame, following the contours. "This building is remarkable."

"If I show you pictures of its original state on the day I signed the papers, you'll faint."

"You renovated?"

"Not personally. My talent with a paintbrush leaves a lot to be desired. I brought in a team of architects and builders to restore it to its original condition. We had a few arguments, especially about soundproofing. They wanted it, I didn't."

"Who won?"

"Guess."

Her smile rivalled the sunshine glinting through the leadlight panes. "When you first opened the college, did you ever see yourself doing this? Just sitting in a room, listening to a single piano?"

Dev rested his head against the wall. "To be completely honest, I had no idea what the future would bring, or even if we'd have a future. I started Perdies with a massive bank loan, a dream, and crossed fingers. Mum has a saying. 'Real life is about choices, and giving yourself permission to fail.' I chose, I gave myself permission, and luckily I didn't fail."

"'Permission to fail' I like that." Katherine put her empty mug to one side, tracing the outline of the painted flowers. "After my parents died, all my choices were taken away from me."

The simple statement hit him with the force of a freight train. He controlled his reaction only with sheer willpower. "What happened to them?"

"Car crash. Wet roads on a dark night. That's the entire story, I'm afraid."

"How old were you?" He kept his voice low and his tone neutral.

"Sixteen." She waved her hand in a dismissive gesture. "Don't worry; I'm not about to subject you to some horrendous tale of abuse and neglect in the welfare system."

He caught her flailing fingers in his. "I'm glad, for you, that is."

"I just meant..." Dev waited, giving her time to gather her thoughts. "I just meant, charity takes away your choices. You're beholden to those people who are doing their best to help, in an overburdened system with little or no resources."

"You didn't have family?"

"Uncles and Aunts. They helped too. Everyone stepped up to the mark. They all did the right thing. Within a year, I was working in a sensible office job I didn't want, living in a sensible flat I didn't like, driving a sensible car I hadn't chosen. I should have been grateful. I *was* grateful for everything they'd done, but the car was *beige*."

Her last word was spoken with such disgust; Dev couldn't help but grin, even as his heart went out to her. "When did you break free?"

"At twenty-one. I traded in the sedan for a snappy yellow hatchback and gave up the job to sing on people's doorsteps."

"My doorstep enjoyed it."

"Maybe it should talk to my uncles and aunts. They still think I'm crazy."

"Wasn't there someone else you could turn to for support, someone special, I mean?" Dev knew he was hinting and couldn't stop himself.

Her smile was rueful. "He didn't understand either."

No wonder she was stubborn. No wonder her hackles rose at the slightest hint of help, or the infamous 'special treatment'.

She tried to pull her hand free. Her body language was tense, was she already regretting the admission shared so unexpectedly? Dev refused to relinquish his hold. He could be stubborn too, especially with gorgeous, fiery, singing kittens he could easily fall in love with. "Listen, it's Chopin's polonaise in A Flat Major. No one plays this like Anna does."

"Don't you have work to do?"

"I'm the boss. I make my own rules."

She resumed her former position, her face turned away from his, the leaded panes highlighting her skin with prisms of colour. Her fingers were cool in his. Dev wanted to keep holding on, to keep her safe, to take away the tragic past that had forged her. He had the power to make some of her shattered dreams come true, and he knew he'd exercise none of it.

"I don't normally tell that story."

"If you're about to apologise, I beg you not to. Perhaps it's this building. Perdies has a way of seeing into people's souls," Dev hunched his shoulders and peered around the room. "Do you think it's haunted?"

"Perhaps you should have had it soundproofed."

"Never. It ruins the acoustics." He went back to listening to the music, relishing the presence of the woman by this side.

With her head tipped upside down, Kat scrubbed at her wet hair with a towel, running through vocal exercise at the same time. The result was a quivery mess of uneven notes. Ditching the towel, she tried again, in an upright position. She paid attention to her posture in the mirror, and to her breathing. This time, the notes rang clear and she gave herself a high five, leaving behind a handprint on the glass. The bathroom practice session was just one of the hundreds of hints she'd picked up in class.

"Warm steam hydrates the throat. A hydrated throat helps the voice." She sung her new mantra to the tune of the latest pop hit, adding some spontaneous dance moves into the mix.

Thank God I live alone. I look like a mad woman.

She grinned at her reflection, shoving the unruly damp hair out of her eyes. Everything she learnt at Perdies was helpful, and informative, and brilliant. The last seven days had been the happiest of her adult life. She couldn't remember ever having such a sense of purpose, of being so eager to embrace every single day.

She was ready and out the door by eight o'clock, dashing past Mrs. Jenkins in the foyer.

"Off to school, my dear?"

"I am."

"You look so happy these days, Katherine."

"I am." Kat threw the words, and a smile, over her shoulder.

Perdies was open, with people already wandering the spacious corridors. The school appeared to have an open-door policy as well as their freeform classes. No matter how early she arrived, someone always beat her to it. Music spilled from somewhere in the building from the moment she stepped inside, to the time she forced herself to leave every night.

And I love it.

She waved to Jules who had the phone receiver pressed to her ear, and chatted to a third-year singer whose advice so far had been invaluable.

Glancing around, she automatically sought Devlin's presence. He'd been away for the last two days, and Kat missed the unique combination of his languorous grace and cheeky smiles as he roamed the halls of the school he so clearly loved.

His office door was closed, meaning he was still away, or in a meeting.

It doesn't matter. He's busy, and so am I.

Kat turned her back on thoughts of Perdies' owner and headed towards her first class of the day.

Twelve hours later, she was tucked up in her favourite spot in the top floor library, pouring over the next book in her must-read pile, a fascinating study of the seven basic elements of music. Strains of piano music drifted to her from along the landing, a poignant, evocative piece. *Moonlight Sonata*. Anna must be practicing again. Kat listened for a few seconds before putting aside her book, wanting a closer vantage point. She almost tripped over something leaning against the doorframe, a familiar silver tipped cane. Peering around, she looked for Devlin. Had the cane been there when she walked into the library? No, surely, she would have noticed. Torn between her usual mix of good manners and insatiable curiosity where Devlin was concerned, she picked up the cane and examined it. The silver head was smooth and worn, tarnished by age, and the palms of its numerous owners. She'd assumed the design was purely decorative, but on closer inspection, she saw it was a lion, a majestic lion's head with a flowing mane, caught in mid growl. A chuckle escaped her. No wonder Devlin felt such a connection to his antique discovery.

Music still streamed along the corridor. With the cane in her hand, she followed the sounds, drawn siren-like by the sheer beauty of Beethoven. She peered into the room, and sure enough, Devlin, not Anna, was the talented artist playing so beautifully. The moon's pale rays were the only light in the room. They flickered around his head and shoulders in fractured shadows, given movement by the immense Jarrah trees that surrounded Perdies on all sides. With his face in profile, he was a vision of beauty, a throwback to another time in history, to when the house was young and new, and the harsh light of electricity didn't even exist. The muscles in his back and shoulders shifted under his white shirt, echoing the movement of his hands. If she had to describe the scene in a single word, Kat would pick *wow*.

"Good evening, Katherine."

She jerked at his voice. "How did you know it was me?"

"I recognised you by the sweet smell of your perfume." He continued playing as he spoke.

"I'm not wearing any."

The jar of a flat note pierced the melodic wall of sound. With a grin, he swung on the stool to face her. "There goes my air of dramatic mystery. To tell you the truth, I saw you sitting in the library. You completely ignored me, so I came in here to play."

He'd been watching her read and she hadn't even noticed? Warmth borne of a desire she wasn't ready to admit to, started at her toes and didn't stop until it reached her head, lingering in a couple of interesting places along the way. "You're playing *Moonlight Sonata* by moonlight. I think you've nailed dramatic mystery."

He turned back to the keys. "What can I say? I was beguiled by the setting, tempted by the moment."

Kat stepped into the room, beguiled by *him*. "I had you pegged as a guitarist."

"I do that too."

"You're full of surprises. Do you sing as well?"

"Enough to carry a tune. Not enough to be a student in my own school. Do you play? I didn't see it on your resume."

Kat's chuckle was self-deprecating. "I'm a self-taught singer who learnt to read music through watching YouTube videos and poring over old sheet music books at my local library. I'm afraid piano lessons weren't in my budget."

His fingers paused mid note. "Do you still want to?"

"Absolutely. Some of my favourite pieces of music are written for piano."

"Great. We'll start now." He leapt up from the stool, plucked the cane from her hand and gestured to the seat, all in one fluid movement.

"Sorry, what?"

"You want to learn. I'm happy to teach."

She stared at him in bemusement. "I'm here at Perdies to improve my singing."

"Show me where it says that on the application form?"

"Devlin, you *cannot* teach me how to play piano."

"I'm not suggesting you could wow them at Carnige Hall, but I bet I can teach you one piece, something simple, and I'll do it in under an hour." He rested both hands on the cane, the challenge in his eyes crystal clear, even through the dappled moonlight bathing them.

"You're crazy."

"I've been called worse."

"Don't you have other things to do?"

"I keep telling you, I'm the boss. Take a seat, Miss Grant, your one-hour lesson is counting down."

Kat perched on the edge of the padded stool still holding the heat from his body. He leaned over from behind, wrapping both arms around her, and placed her hands on the keys, adjusting her fingers until he had them exactly where he wanted. His proximity was intoxicating, that subtle aftershave—or whatever it was—tantalised her senses. When he pressed down on her fingers, the resulting chord startled her. He did it again, and again, six times in total. Just enough time for her to figure out the simple tune.

"Chopsticks? Seriously?" she turned her face towards his, which gave her an uber close-up of his strong jaw and evening stubble.

"Technically, it's called '*The Chop Waltz.*'" He moved her fingers to the next chord, and repeated the six bars.

"Even I could work out how to play Chopsticks without tuition."

"And deprive yourself of my teaching skills? I don't come cheap, you know."

"My probationary period covers all tuition free of charge."

"Do you want to argue? Or play."

"Play." She breathed in his unique fragrance, surrendering to the moment, relishing it.

When the mini lesson was over, a mere minute later, he stood back, depriving her of his body warmth. "Scoot over," he plonked down next to her.

Kat wriggled to the edge of the small, square seat. "This isn't a two-person stool, you know."

"We can't play a duet with me standing."

"What duet?"

"The one I'm about to teach you. You've clearly mastered Chopsticks, let's move on to something more challenging. How do you feel about Handel?"

The following hour passed in a blur of laughter and fun...and frustration as it turned out Kat *wasn't* a natural pianist.

"No, it's fine, you almost had it that time, here," he jumped up, and resumed his position at her back, guiding her fingers as he'd done numerous times in the last hour to the point where it felt natural to have his arms around her. "There you go, now you've got it. Let's take it from that last section again," He squeezed onto his half of the stool, his thigh pressed hard against hers, and played. Kat took a deep breath, rolled her shoulders, and focussed on the rhythm and timing. On the third attempt, she got through the entire two-minute piece without a single error.

"Yes!" she raised both hands in the air in triumph.

Devlin looked at his watch. "One hour exactly. I told you so."

Kat rolled her eyes at his smug tone. "Fine, you're brilliant and a genius."

"And you are amazing." He tucked a wayward curl behind her ear.

The atmosphere changed in a heartbeat, morphing from laughter filled, innocent fun, into something decidedly more heated. Moonlight was still their only illumination, but now it carried a subtle energy, wrapping them in its power.

"I'm taking up too much of your time."

"No, you're not." His fingers lingered in her hair.

"You—your cane has a lion's head."

"Your pencil case has *Hello Kitty* pictures on it."

How on earth did he know that? "You *have* been spying on me."

His familiar grin was all knowing and mischief filled, releasing some of the tension from the desire laden cocoon surrounding them.

"You left it in the kitchen. It's why I came looking for you, to return it." He pointed to the side table by the door, where her pencil case was sitting. He moved closer, until she could feel his warm breath against her ear. "Thank you for leaving it in the kitchen. I enjoyed our lesson."

Before she could reply, he stood, stretching his arms above the doorframe with a groan. His phone beeped a message, eliciting a second, louder groan.

"You should get that."

"I don't want to. I've been stuck in meetings in Sydney for the last few days, going quietly insane, and I have to do the same thing next week. Hey, I have an idea. You can come with me, and sing my answers, telegram style."

The phone stopped beeping and started ringing, meaning their time together was over for now. Kat closed the piano lid and, gave him a haughty sniff. "I don't do singing telegrams anymore, I'm a serious musician now."

"Not even the cute kitten?"

"Nope." Kat squeezed past him, reclaiming her pencil case on the way, and managing *not* to brush against his torso which relieved and disappointed her in equal measures.

"Sexy Stewardess?"

"Not a chance," she tossed the comment over her shoulder as she headed to the library to grab her handbag.

"Naughty Nun?" his tone was so hopeful, Kat bit back a giggle.

He was framed in the doorway, backlit by the moon.

Funny how we hadn't bothered turning on the light.

At some point in the impromptu tuition, he'd rolled up his shirt sleeves and ditched the tie, giving him that familiar dishevelled look she found so irresistible. Kat drank in the sight of him for another second, before starting down the stairs. "Keep dreaming, Mr. Perdie."

"I will, Miss Grant. I promise you, I will."

Chapter Four

Dev paused in the middle of reading a contract to listen to the sounds of his school. After another three-day interstate trip, he'd missed its atmosphere. From the ground floor came a strong bass baritone. His second-year student, a divorced father of three, had a great future ahead. Dev would bet money on him singing on the world stage within three years.

The complex violin concerto drifted through his open office window, jarred by a wrong note and a litany of four-letter words from the violinist in question practicing his craft in the afternoon sunshine.

I feel like I'm surrounded by music. It's like I've come home. Katherine was right. She understood this place. Perdies lived and breathed its music, embraced, and protected its musicians. *You've created something special here.*

He had, and he intended to keep it, regardless of the cost.

Right on cue, another voice joined the mix, Katherine, singing a catchy pop number. He knew it was her. He'd pick her voice out of dozens, hundreds, thousands. Dev closed his eyes, focusing on every note, every breath. Two weeks of her probation had passed already. Two perfect, incredible, torturous weeks of watching her confidence grow and her talent fly.

"Hey, boss. Want a coffee?"

Dev sat up straighter in his chair, pushing aside the hum of desire Katherine's voice always awakened in him. "Make it a double."

Jules smile was altogether too smug. "She's got a great set of pipes, hasn't she?"

"I have no idea who you're talking about."

"Sure, you don't. Do you want your phone messages now or later?"

"Now is fine."

"The ABC are asking for a radio interview. I gave them a tentative maybe. Your brothers want to remind you about the new car you promised them if they aced their latest exams. The vet called about Evita."

Devlin held his hand out for the last message, ignoring the others. He was dialling even before Jules left the room.

"Mr. Jones, thank you for calling back. Evita had two teeth removed, and is just coming out of the anaesthetic now. She'll need antibiotics, but should be fine." The vet's voice was calm and reassuring.

The knot of anxiety in the centre of Dev's chest dissolved. "That's it? That's why she's been off her food?"

"No one wants to eat with a toothache."

His relief was tempered by the vet's next question. "I see Othello is due for his next appointment. Do you wish to make that now?"

"I... I'm in and out of the state for the next few weeks. I'll make a time soon, I promise. With regards to Evita, when can I collect her?"

"Give her an hour, and she'll be ready to go home."

"Thanks, that's great. I'll be there shortly." He stood, and took a turn around his office, rolling the tension from his shoulders.

Jules returned with his coffee. "Good news?"

"Yep. Toothache."

"You worry too much about those animals." Jules was *not* a cat person.

He shrugged off her familiar disinterest. "I'm skipping out early today. Hold the fort for me?"

"I always do. By the way, all the newbies, and some of the seniors went out last night."

Dev halted by the door. "They did?"

"I hear karaoke was involved."

The thought of Katherine singing in a pub surrounded by friends made him smile.

"From what I saw this morning, some of them are pretty hungover."

"Getting prudish in your old age, Jules?"

"Just hoping I don't have to clean up any vomit. If I do, I'm charging you triple rates. A couple of the seniors were chatting in the kitchen. One said he's trying to get up the courage to ask Kat out for dinner after he heard her karaoke version of Adele. Just saying, boss, she's gorgeous, and talented. Someone's going to fall in love with her. Someone *else*, I mean." Jules shot him a meaningful look. "On an unrelated matter, she's upstairs in Room 8, in case you're interested, having a one-on-one session."

"Evita? I thought she was at the vets."

"Funny. You can't fool me. I've known you too long."

"Katherine Grant is a student."

"You're twenty-eight, she's twenty-five. Do something, you idiot, before it's too late."

"Stop being logical, or I'll make you house sit all my cats next week while I'm in Melbourne."

Dev was halfway out of the building before he turned back, and found himself outside Room 8, after a quick detour to the kitchen, lured by Katherine's siren song.

"Hi, Dev." Phil, one of his most senior voice coaches was rummaging through a pile of sheet music. "Have you come to see our star student? She's done remarkably well."

"I know. I've been listening. May I?" he gestured to the piano.

"We're almost finished. I'm happy to grab a cuppa if you want to take over the rest of the lesson."

"Fine by me. What about you, Katherine?"

Her nod of agreement didn't match the suspicious look in her eyes. Once they were alone, he handed her the tea. "I thought you might need this, after all the singing last night."

A flush of colour highlighted her cheeks as she cradled the cup in her hands. "You heard about that."

"Of course."

"Are we in trouble?"

His surprised laugh was genuine. "Katherine, I'm running a music school, not a high school. Did you have a good time?"

She took a few sips before speaking, as if unsure of the answer. "It was childish, and silly, and... fun."

Dev's heart went out to her. How much had she missed in her teenage years? The rites of passage others took for granted. "You don't sound croaky, and you don't look hungover."

"I'm neither, although I can't say the same for some of the others."

"Yes, I saw a few wilted souls in the kitchen trying to hook up in intravenous drip to the coffee machine." His quip brought a smile to her lips. He sat at the piano stool and ran his fingers over the keys. "Here we are again."

"You actually teach your students?"

"When the mood takes me."

"So, it's not just me?"

"Of course not. No special treatment." He picked up the pile of music. "Do you have any requests for a song? Adele's latest masterpiece, perhaps?"

"Is there *anything* you don't know about last night?"

"I know I'm sorry I missed it. Pick a song, Katherine, unless you'd rather another piano duet."

"We're in school hours, I'll stick to vocals."

"If you insist."

"Isn't it the teacher's job to decide what I sing?"

"Alright. I never asked. What were you supposed to be performing on the day of your probationary interview? Judging by the outfit, I'm guessing it was something to do with planes?"

"*'Come Fly With Me.'*"

"Ah, Frank Sinatra. I don't have that one. I do, however, have this."

She glanced at the sheet music for *Memory* he held up for approval. "We've already had this discussion."

"You're spoiling all my fun, Miss Grant."

She bent to whisper in his ear, her breath a warm sweep of air on his skin. "You're not being very professional, Mr. Perdie."

Ignoring the rush of awareness caused by her proximity, he handed her another sheet. "How do you feel about '*Stand By Your Man*?'"

He was rewarded with a smile she was clearly struggling to hide. "It's very melancholy."

"Perhaps I'm in melancholy mood." Dev hit a note on the piano. "Go up one key, I want to test your range. Unless it's too much of a challenge."

"I relish challenges."

"Good, and we even have a two-person stool." He patted the space beside him, fully expecting her to refuse. Had the intimacy he'd felt last week at another piano been in his imagination? Had the connection been all in his head?

To his surprise, she sat, propping up the music so they could share. "Bring it on, Maestro."

After a six-bar intro, she began to sing, and the rest of Dev's world ceased to exist. No, not just the world, the entire universe coalesced into just the two of them. The acoustics in the music room were pitch perfect, as was her voice. It resonated and swirled around him. Dev didn't bother with the sheet music. He played by ear, unable to take his eyes off her.

When the final note hung in the air, he drank in her half-parted lips, the pulse beating in her throat. God, this wasn't in his head. Nothing had ever felt so real, so *right*. In an almost unconscious movement, he reached up and touched the flush of colour high on her cheek. "Kat."

A loud clapping ripped through the intensity of the moment. Dev dropped his hand as half of Perdies, including teachers and students had gathered in the doorway.

"Well done."

"Oh my God, that was amazing."

"You almost made me cry."

The compliments were almost undistinguishable as everyone tried to talk at once. With colour still staining her cheeks, Katherine jumped up from the stool, bobbing a neat curtsey to the crowd. The chatter continued as more probation students spilled into the room for the next group lesson.

This was *not* the time to discuss connections and feelings. Katherine needed to be with her friends, people who admired and loved her, *apart from me*. And he had a semi-conscious cat to collect and a vet bill to pay. Dev decided on a discreet getaway. Phil slapped him on the back in passing. "I told you she was good."

"I never doubted it for a moment."

"You two should be a duet."

"I can't think of anything more perfect."

"Evita, sweetheart, you can stop yowling now. We're home." She ignored him, keeping up the chorus of complaint as Dev shouldered open the door, juggling his briefcase and the cat cage in one hand.

As soon as he lifted the cage's latch, his outraged pet shot out like a bullet, giving him an angry swish of her tail. Her indignant mood only increased after dinner when he squirted a dose of foul-smelling antibiotic paste into her mouth.

Carmen joined her housemate in feline solidarity. The two of them curled up by the fire, indulging in a lengthy bout of mutual grooming and giving their human slave the occasional withering glare.

Knowing he'd be forgiven for his actions in a day or two, Dev scooped Othello from his favourite spot by the window and carried him to the sofa. "As the only other male in the house, we need to stick together. Someone has to be on my side."

Othello responded by tucking his head under Devlin's chin, his rumbling purr vibrating the very walls around them. Othello was a cuddle junky from *way* back. Relaxing into the deep sofa with a sigh, Dev stroked the soft fur. "I need some advice about Katherine. What do I do with a tenacious, gorgeous woman who has every reason not to want my help? I've tried giving her space, being professional and keeping everything on a businesslike level. She likes my tea, *that* much I know. Maybe I should give up on Perdies and hire myself as a barista. We could work together in a café. Do you think that would work?" Dev huffed out a breath. "What I really want is to take her out, for dinner, or coffee, or long walks on the beach, or whatever the hell normal people do when they find someone they want to be with."

What did he know about normal? The last time he'd been on a date was so long ago, monasteries around the world would welcome him into their cloisters with open arms.

The current probation period ended in six weeks, and he'd be interstate for at least half of it. Dammit, the timing sucked. At least after that he'd know. Either, Katherine would get accepted as a full time Perdies student, and he'd see her every single day. Or, she wouldn't make the cut, and disappear from his life forever. The mere thought of that made Dev's heart clench.

"She deserves a chance to live her dream, and make it happen on her own terms." Memories of her voice, her smile, the flash of fire in her eyes when she was angry, played through his mind like a slide show. "I'm falling for her, Othello. She's brilliant, she's funny. She's... everything."

Othello responded to the lack of stroking by head-butting him in the chin.

Dev chuckled, even as his teeth came together with a painful snap. He kissed the greying fur on Othello's head, and scratched the spot just behind his ear. "Yeah, buddy. I love you too."

Kat sprinted from her car, waving to the musicians practicing under the shelter of the pergola. Only at Perdies would you see a string quartet, wearing jeans and T-shirt, rehearsing outside in the rain.

That's why I love this place so much.

The declaration brought her up short, despite the raindrops landing on her shoes.

I love this place.

For the past nine years she'd avoided getting too attached to anything, or anyone. Some people, like Gino, had wormed their way under her defensive barriers, past the protective shields of her tentative heart. This was different, much more powerful. She was at home here, at peace.

What about Devlin?

The thought arrived unbidden.

Yes, Perdies owner was a real part of that peace, that sense of true belonging for the first time in her adult life. Kat swallowed against the tide of emotion the realisation produced.

He isn't mine. I can't claim him.

Yet another thought followed the first, an unsettling thought about Devlin's continuous absence and constant meetings. Was Perdies in financial trouble? Was that the reason for his frenetic schedule, the continuous barrage of phone calls and closed-door conferences? During her short stint as an office worker, she'd seen businesses shut their doors despite their owners' frantic efforts to save them. Was it possible the beautiful music school she loved so much was soon to be another victim of a changing world? The mere thought of losing something so precious was a physical pain in her chest.

A drop of moisture dripped from the end of her umbrella onto her nose, making her grimace. Earth shattering, light bulb moments, and worrisome thoughts could wait, at least until she was out of the rain.

"Shut the door."

Devlin's bellowed command reverberated along the long hallway with such intensity Kat was certain both her feet left the floor. She slammed the door behind her and leaned against it, just as a flash of white flew past and up the staircase.

"Grab her!"

"Who?"

"The cat. Grab the cat." Devlin tore up the stairs, his footsteps pounding on the jarrah treads.

Dropping everything, Kat took off after them, almost careering into Devlin's body when he stopped without warning. "Which way did she go?"

"I didn't see."

He jerked his thumb toward a smaller music room. "You go left. I'll go right."

"Who am I looking for?"

"Evita. You can try calling her name, but she'll probably ignore you." The information was tossed over his shoulder as he disappeared through the open door of the office opposite.

Kat peered into the empty room. "Evita? Puss puss. Here, Evita."

"I've got her... wait, Evita, *wait.* Bloody hell!" Devlin flew past her and back down the stairs. Biting back laughter, Kat followed, a confused participant in a bizarre congo line.

Tom let out a startled squeak and clutched his flute to his chest as they tore past.

Evita slid and slipped on the marble floor as her paws tried to find traction. With that natural agility known only to felines, she darted under side tables and chairs, evading Devlin's grabbing hands. He cursed under his breath as she tried to double back, heading towards the stairs again.

Kat stepped into her way, waving her hands back and forth, and she did an about face, paws moving at double speed.

"That's it. Herd her in this direction." Devlin scrambled to his feet, having half crawled under a table to reach her.

The iconic phrase *herding cats* had never been so apt. She mustn't laugh. Despite the incongruous situation, Devlin was clearly not amused.

He let out a cry of triumph when the lightning-fast feline bolted into his office. "Quick. Get the door."

Kat was right on his heels, wrenching the door closed behind her.

"Ha. Now we've got you. Come on, Evita. This is for your own good." His voice was muffled as he dropped to his knees to look under the couch, giving Kat an impressive view of well-toned buttocks.

"What is?" Kat cleared her throat as the words came out huskier than she intended.

"Antibiotic paste. She hates taking it, and I don't blame her. The stuff smells revolting."

"Wouldn't it be easier to do at home?"

"She needs four doses a day and I had meetings I couldn't cancel."

That explained the cat travel cage sitting in the corner of the room. A flicker of movement caught her eye. "Devlin, look. Behind the curtain."

He flung back the heavy drapes and sure enough, Evita shot out. "Grab her."

They dove for the underside of Devlin's mahogany desk from opposite ends, meeting in the middle with a wince inducing clash of heads.

Kat rubbed at her throbbing forehead, fighting back giggles. "Ouch, Devlin, your head is *hard*."

She expected him to join in, or come up with some witty comment. Instead, he did something totally unexpected. Devlin kissed her.

The circumstances weren't ideal as they were crouched on all fours on the floor, yet somehow, he made it work. His lips were soft, warm, and inviting. Only the faintest hint of stubble grazed her skin.

"God, you're so beautiful." The words were a murmur of sound against her mouth, the intensity in them creating a shiver of sensation along her nerve endings.

"Dev, are we still on for this arvo?" At the unfamiliar voice, and the squeak of a door handle, Kat pulled her lips free and scrambled backwards on hands and knees.

"Wait a sec." Devlin did the same, lunging for the door as it opened.

Kat scanned the room, desperate for an escape route. She spied the ever-resourceful Evita scratching at the door to some sort of built in cupboard. Scooping her up on the way, Kat pulled the narrow door fully open and slipped inside. She jerked as her head hit a row of metal coat hangers hanging on a rail in the large space, making them jangle. *Coat hangers?* Wait, this wasn't a cupboard, it was a wardrobe.

"Katherine?" the puzzled tone of Devlin's voice was clear despite the wooden barrier separating them. "Katherine? Where did you go? Evita?"

His pet *finally* responded to her name with a disgruntled meow.

A mere second later, Kat blinked against the light as the wardrobe door reopened.

Devlin leaned against the jamb, enjoyment dancing in his eyes. "Hello, Katherine. I can't wait for this explanation."

"Shut up. It was the only escape route I could find at short notice."

He peered into the darkened space. "You do know it's just a wardrobe, right? It doesn't lead to Narnia."

"It might. I have a lion." She held up Evita for his inspection.

"Why are you hiding, exactly?"

"So, it didn't look suspicious."

"As opposed to the damning scenario of you, 'being in my office helping to look for my cat' you mean?"

Just because she had her arms full, didn't mean she couldn't kick him. She aimed for his shins, missing as he side-stepped her efforts with his usual agile grace. "I panicked, okay? You were *kissing* me."

Unease replaced the amusement on his face. "I scared you?"

"Of course not. I liked it." The words were out before she could stop them.

"Good." He stepped into the space, shutting the door behind him, rendering the small space pitch black.

"What... what are you doing?" her words ended on a soprano high note.

"Panicking, and kissing you."

Despite the darkness, he found her mouth with unerring accuracy on the first attempt. With the cat still in her arms, full body contact was impossible. There were only his lips on hers, one arm curled around her waist. Technically, the kiss was chaste.

Yeah, right.

On a scale of one to ten it registered a definite eleven.

"How... how are you doing that?"

"What? I have a confession to make, I *have* kissed women before. Admittedly, the wardrobe aspect is original."

"No, I mean, how are you aiming? I can't see a thing. Why aren't you licking my eyeball or sucking on my nose?"

His chuckle surrounded her, heating her from the inside, setting off little sparks of electricity throughout her body. "Katherine, my sweet, are you going to bring this level of romance to *all* our intimate encounters?"

Intimate encounters.

The phrase was enough to make her shiver in anticipation. Katherine struggled to form a coherent thought. "I'm just saying, this is crazy. We're in your office."

Devlin traced feather light kisses along her neck. "I consider this room to be neutral territory."

"First it's not-Narnia and now it's Switzerland? Does your wardrobe know it has a personality disorder?"

Okay, that chuckle of his was highly addictive, and those body wide electric sparks were zeroing in on some *highly* sensitive spots.

"Will you hit me if I admit something? I've wanted to do this since the first moment I laid eyes on you," he said.

"On your doorstep?"

"Yep. Standing there with your whiskers and kitten ears, seducing me with your voice."

"I was *not* seducing you."

"Not intentionally, I know." He turned his attention to her earlobe.

With her sight stolen, all the others senses clicked into high gear. The feel of her heartbeat hammering in her chest. The touch of Devlin's hand on her hip, his fingertips grazing the skin as they slid under her shirt. The sound of his increased breathing as he claimed her lips in another fleeting, achingly evocative kiss. One kiss turned into two, three, four, she lost count after that. There was only the powerful sense of him in the darkness, an impossible intimacy.

Evita's purring penetrated the haze of desire, bringing a smile to Kat's lips still pressed to his. "I think she's asleep."

"Of course. *Now* she's happy to stay in one place." Devlin's resigned tone, spoken in a low murmur, wound the bonds of closeness around them even tighter, a shared moment of understanding, amid desire and chaos.

Devlin traced his finger along her lips. "I want to stay here."

"Forever?"

"Totally. We'll put in plumbing, and I'll arrange for room service."

How could he arouse her and make her laugh all at the same time? "You'll be missed."

"I don't care. Unfortunately, I'm expected in a meeting, and our unwanted visitors will be returning any minute." With an obvious reluctance, he took a step back, nudging the door open and spilling unwelcome light into their hiding place. Even though they'd barely been touching, losing physical contact was heart wrenching.

Kat peered at the heavy wooden door as he closed it behind them. "Why do you even have a wardrobe in your office?"

"It used to be the master bedroom."

For some idiotic reason, the thought of kissing him for the very first time in a bedroom made the whole peculiar situation way more intimate.

Devlin took Evita from her arms. "Katherine, are you blushing?"

"No."

"You painted your cheeks red in the last five seconds without me noticing?"

"Stop teasing me."

"You leave me no option. We're back to kissing."

A second knock at the door had them springing apart. "Dev, are you ready for this meeting? Oh, sorry."

"It's fine, I was just... helping Mr Perdie find his cat." Kat ducked her head at Devlin's grin.

"I would never have found her without you. Thanks for the help, Miss Grant. Regarding that matter we discussed, can we pick it up later?"

"I'm sure we can." She fled, with burning cheeks, and the weight of Devlin's stare on her back.

Chapter Five

"Did you say something, Kat?"

She bolted upright in her chair, shuffling under the gaze of her teacher like a guilty ten-year-old. "What? Sorry? No... no I'm sure I didn't. What were we discussing?"

"The climax of tension."

"Climax?" Sniggers reverberated around the class, not surprising, considering her exclamation had come out more like a shrill yelp.

"It's a melodic theory whereby a series of tones sound in succession, typically moving towards a climax of tension before resolving to a state of rest."

As the entire class surrendered to outright laughter, the teacher rolled her eyes. "Alright, you lot, I know what you're thinking. Not everything is about sex, you know."

"That's a shame," someone called out from the back.

At least she wasn't the only one in a double entendre mindset. After the wardrobe encounter, Kat's brain was on a one-way street to desire and pure, unadulterated lust. Focussing on her numerous classes was taking all her concentration, and then some.

God, you're so beautiful.

I've wanted to do this since the first moment I laid eyes on you.

Arousal sent a shiver along her spine, which, considering her current location, was *not* in keeping with her academic professionalism.

She'd kissed him. She'd actually kissed him.

"Kat?"

Kat dragged her attention back to the classroom to find everyone staring at her. Oh God, had she said something out loud?

The teacher gave her a sympathetic look. "It's okay, it's been a busy week, especially for our newbies. Why don't we call it a day? Everyone, please note the websites on the whiteboard, and if anyone has questions, remember, you can always text me."

The students shuffled out, chatting among themselves. "Hey, Kat, you okay?" Ava asked as she retrieved her cello from the hallway for her next class.

"Fine, thank you."

"We're going out for drinks tonight, you've been throwing yourself into study, why don't you come?"

"Not this time," Kat glanced at her watch, "I promised my boss I'd do a shift at the café. I've been neglecting him and spending all my time here."

"It's great, isn't it?" Ava glanced around, hugging her cello to her chest like an oversized fluffy toy. "I love everything about this place."

"Yeah, so do I," *and I kissed the owner*. Kat's gaze strayed to Devlin's closed office door.

Her concentration didn't improve during her three-hour shift at Gino's. But at least it was a distraction. The place was bustling, filled with caffeinated uni students cramming for upcoming exams. Kat had to move around books piled on tables to find room for the food and endless cups of coffee.

"Three more serves of fries for table nine." Gino shoved them into her hands. "And two expressos for table six after that."

"Got it." She juggled the steaming hot baskets, her mouth watering at the delicious aroma of fresh hot chips. Dodging customers, and wriggling between tables kept her busy, meaning her shift flew by. Thoughts of a sexy, delicious, wardrobe kissing cat lover were lost under the onslaught of cakes, chips, and coke orders.

Uni students needed to seriously improve their diets.

Gino nudged her with his elbow when she returned to the kitchen for the umpteenth time. "Here, take this cake to your favourite customers, they're looking stressed."

Sure enough, the twins were sitting in a corner booth, almost hidden by the enormous pile of text books and the two laptops propped up in front of them. Kat took the giant wedge of cheesecake and two spoons with a grin and headed over. "Gino thought you might need this."

They peered at her with bloodshot eyes, fatigue written all over their faces.

"You're a star."

"A total star."

"A galaxy of stars."

"Dude, I already have the star thing covered, pick another metaphor."

"I can't. I'm too tired."

Kat chuckled at the familiar high-speed monologue as she cleared away the excess coffee cups and food plates and returned with two glasses of water. "Drink these. You can't live on coffee, it's bad for you."

"Tell that to our teachers. They're killing us, Kat, literally killing us."

She perched her hip on the edge of the desk. "I know, I'm a student now as well, remember?"

"I bet you're nailing it, right?"

"Totally nailing it."

Memories of Devlin's mouth on hers assaulted her senses with a visceral slideshow. "It's great. I love it, every minute of every day."

"We knew you would. You're awesome."

"Totally awesome."

"Awesome plus."

"Dude, stop stealing my words."

"Shut up, my brain's fried."

Kat pushed the water towards them as a gentle hint. "It'll all be worth it when you pass."

"Mum's taking us to Europe if we get A's on every exam."

"Europe? Wow, how lucky are you two? That's one heck of a generous mum."

"Our brother's helping. He's cool."

"Super cool. I mean, really, *really* cool. He's promised to buy us a car." They both stared at her in expectation. Clearly, they *really* loved their family. Kat wondered if the twins ever added up how many times they used the word 'really' in an average day.

"If I had brothers, I'd like them to be just like you."

They exchanged a glance. "Do you mean that?"

"Really mean that?"

"I really do. You'll have to wear name tags, so I can tell you apart."

"We will."

"Totally will." They high fived, their whoops echoing around the café. God, they were funny.

Gino beckoned her from the kitchen. Kat gathered the last of the plates and waved them a quick goodbye.

"Duty calls, and you need to get back to your study. Good luck on the exams. Fingers crossed for Europe."

"We're stoked that you're happy, Kat."

"Really happy."

"Happy plus."

"Seriously, bro, find your own words, why don't you?"

"I will, *after* the exams."

The brief, but enjoyable exchange with the twins pushed away her own tiredness, as it always did, and gave her the energy to finish her shift without thinking of Devlin… for five seconds at a time, anyway.

By the time she got home, she only had time to polish off the last of the chips Gino had kindly donated, before collapsing into bed. "I kissed him." The words were the last thing she remembered, before diving into sleep, where dreams of warm kisses in darkened spaces chased her throughout the night.

He'd kissed her. Kissed her and promptly ignored her for twenty-four hours straight. That's what his feisty little kitten will be assuming, anyway. Dev glared at his ringing phone, willing it to stop, preferably to vanish into thin air. “Five minutes. All I’m asking for is five bloody minutes of peace.”

Jules poked her head around the door. “You know it’s not sentient, right. You press that little green button in the shape of a phone.”

“Can’t you take messages for the next five hours?” The look he sent her was openly pleading.

“Sure, then I’ll add the messages to these messages and you can have an even bigger backlog than you do now.” She held out the square pieces of paper in her hand.

Dev slumped back in his chair. “Has Katherine arrived yet?”

“It’s seven thirty in the morning. I’m assuming she has a life outside of school even if you don’t. Hang on, *I’m* here, when did my life disappear?” her smile softened the horrified tone of her words.

“You know how much I appreciate you.”

“That’s good, boss, because I’m giving myself a pay rise next week.”

"If you see Katherine, could you let me know?" Dev eyed the cane resting against his desk. "Wait, I have a better idea. I'll be back in a sec."

He ignored Jules' resigned sigh and the sound of his phone starting to ring again, as he snatched up the cane and raced up the stairs to the top floor library.

As usual it was deserted. Most of the students preferred to download their study material as e-books. It seemed only he and Katherine relished the simple pleasure of reading the old-fashioned way. Dev propped the cane up just outside the door. "Come and find me, Katherine, my arms are aching to hold you."

By the time he'd swam his way through meetings and phone calls yesterday, she'd left. Dev's entire night was spent in memory of exquisite kisses and the silky touch of her skin.

"Boss, your phone is ringing off the hook and I'm about to throw it out the window." Devlin winced as his sensual recollections were shattered by Jules bellowing up the stairwell.

"Coming."

An hour later, he jumped up from his desk in anticipation as his office door opened. His disappointment was tempered by genuine happiness at the welcome sight of a former student hovering on the threshold. “Pippa? What are you doing in this neck of the woods?”

“Hi, Dev. Sorry, I probably shouldn’t barge in like this, Jules wasn’t at her desk,” she gestured behind her.

“I think I saw her running down the street screaming a few minutes ago, it’s been busy.”

“When are you ever *not* busy? I wanted to show you something.” She held up the typed page in her hands.

Dev left his desk for a better look. “Is that... is that a recording contract?”

Her enthusiastic nod and smile answered his question without words.

“Pippa, that’s brilliant news, I’m so happy for you.”

“I could never have done it without you.” Pippa surprised him by throwing her arms around his neck.

Considering the way their relationship had progressed so far, Dev shouldn’t have been surprised when Katherine chose that precise instant to walk into his office. Like a movie cliché, everything slowed down, the next few seconds lasted an eternity as the cane slid from her fingers to hit the ground with a loud, echoing crack. The silver head broke off, spinning in the air to land some distance away, leaving the wooden stick lying on the ground.

The look of shame, horror and hurt on Katherine's face was too much for him to take. When time reverted to its normal speed, Dev lunged for her, just as she turned on her heel to run.

"Oh no you don't, not this time." He caught her by the wrist before she had a chance to bolt.

"I shouldn't have come in. I should have knocked."

"Don't be an idiot, why do you think I left the cane?"

"Let me go, you're obviously *busy*." Her acerbic tone couldn't mask the pain behind it.

"Will you stop wriggling, you're worse than my cats." He solved the problem by hauling her towards him and enfolding both arms around her waist, spinning them both to face Pippa. "Katherine, sweetheart, I know power walking is our thing, but can we skip the cardio workout for today? At least until I give you an explanation."

"You don't owe me anything." She was still squirming, and being as her back was pressed against the entire front of him, his body's physical reaction was inevitable... and embarrassing, considering they weren't alone.

Down, boy.

"Pippa, this is Katherine. She and I are seeing each other, or we will be, as soon as she admits to it. You should also know, she has a tendency to jump to ludicrous conclusions. She's the only person I know who can put two and two together and come up with one million, six hundred and thirty-seven—ouch." Dev's monologue ended with a wince as Katherine kicked backwards, hitting him in the shin.

"Hi." Pippa's expression was a mixture of amusement and confusion.

"If you could tell Katherine what you just told me, I'd appreciate it, preferably before I pass out from agony."

His former student held up the paper in her hand. "I have a recording contract. It's a tiny, independent label in Sydney and I'll probably only sell fifty copies, but I don't care. They're *my* songs, originals, not covers. I came by to say thank you to Devlin and to Perdies for taking a chance on me."

"Pippa was one of our first applicants when we first opened our doors and she became our first graduate.

She was there at the start, when Perdies was new and we had no idea what we were doing."

"You... you dated?" Katherine's question was hesitant.

Dev was saved from answering when Pippa burst out laughing. "Dated? God, no. No offense, Dev, you're not my type."

"None taken."

"That's my other bit of news. I'm engaged." She held up her left hand, fingers splayed to show off the sparkling ring on her fourth finger.

"In that case, congratulations twice over. You deserve this, Pippa, you've worked hard for it."

Pippa looked around his office. "This place changed my life. I owe everything to you, Dev. Sorry for the interruption. I guess my timing was off."

Dev tightened his arms around Katherine. "Timing is something we're still working on." She was quiet and unmoving in his arms. He could let go, except he didn't want to, not while her warm body was pressed to his, not while the tips of his fingers were brushing against the skin of her abdomen where the T-shirt had ridden up during her squirming. It took all his willpower not to nuzzle the side of her neck.

"Hi Pippa, I didn't know you were in town, great to see you." Jules strode into the office carrying two mugs. She glanced at him, a smile tugging up the corner of her mouth. "I see you found Kat. I take it you want this office to be an interrupt free zone for a while?"

"Half an hour at the very least. No phone calls, no meetings, no visitors unless the building is burning down, and even then, I'd rather you try and put it out yourself first."

"Consider it done. C'mon, Pippa, let's leave the lovebirds alone. You can tell me all your news, especially about that giant rock on your finger."

As soon as the door closed behind them, Dev released Katherine, just enough to turn her around to face him. "Hi."

"I broke your cane." Her words were blurted out at high speed.

Kissing seemed to solve her worried expression, so he did, and just like before, everything else faded away. This was the real thing. No cats, no cramped spaces, no bashing of heads. Just the sublime pleasure of her body pressed to his, the erotic sensuality of her mouth, warm and soft.

The gentle, almost teasing caress intensified in a heartbeat. Somehow, he ended up with the wall at his back. How had they gotten here? He neither knew, nor cared. His little kitten was in control now, biting at his lips, trailing her hands along his ribcage, and upwards, across his shoulders. True to her nature, when she applied herself, it was at full speed, one hundred and ten percent, sheer determination, and God, he loved her for it. She was beautiful, passionate, and *alive*. He cradled her face in his hands, driven crazy by the hitches in her breathing, the whispered sighs absorbed by his kisses. She tugged at his shirt, yanking it from his pants until she found the skin beneath. Now it was Dev's turn to moan, as the scrape of her nails sent a bolt of pure lust along his nerve endings.

He tore his mouth from hers, just so he could plant kisses along her neck, biting at the sensitive chords and loving the way her body jerked and shivered. "You know we're dating now, right?"

"Shut up, Devlin."

"I'm just making sure you know, given your tendency for misunderstandings."

"We'll discuss it later."

"Now seems a good time—" he broke off when she pushed her thigh between his and pressed against his arousal. It was either a sensual caress, or a warning of imminent pain. Dev decided to play it safe. "Okay, got it, we'll talk later."

At some point his mobile rang. He ignored it. Nothing was more important than the woman in his arms, seducing him with every touch, every breath from her lips.

The phone screamed at him a second, then third time. He should have given that damn mobile to Jules. It stopped, after some time, but he knew the reprieve was a short one. With a great deal of reluctance, Dev lifted his mouth from Katherine's.

We never have enough time, little kitten.

"Someone is really keen to talk to you today." She tried to pull away. He stopped her by linking his fingers at the small of her back.

"Have dinner with me."

"It's nine o'clock in the morning."

"Must you confuse everything with logic? I meant later, at dinner time. I thought about you all last night. You don't know how many times I almost called."

"Why didn't you?"

"I didn't have your number, and yes, before you say anything, I could have gotten it from the system, but that meant *taking*. I wanted you to *give* it to me of your own accord."

"I'll give you my number."

"Thank you." He tickled the base of her spine. The quiver that ran through her body telling him that spot was a personal erogenous zone.

Good to know.

"Umm, I might have overreacted when I saw Pippa in your arms. She must think I'm a madwoman."

"Jules will set her straight." Dev fixed her with a mock stare. "So, you assumed I had a continuous stream of girlfriends in and out of my office for hanky-panky? That's not how this works, Miss Grant, I'm sure I said that before."

She controlled a grin with obvious effort. "Is the term hanky-panky still in current use?"

"I was being discreet."

Stroking a sensual path along his neck, she paused only to fiddle with the twisted mass of his tie. "And, I may have pounced on you."

"*May* have?"

"You disapprove?"

"Are you kidding? I love that pounce technique. You should patent it."

When his phone rang for the fourth time and a fifth, she stepped back. "Devlin, get that."

God, this was torture.

Dev turned away, and concentrated on tucking his shirt back into his pants, *and* reciting the periodic table on a loop until his aroused body responded to his pleas for mercy.

"I broke your cane." Katherine had retrieved the two halves. The silver lion head section was reduced to a short, dangerous looking shard.

"It wasn't your fault. It was old, Katherine." When Dev slid a consoling arm around her waist, she responded by resting her head on his shoulder. That simple act, of seeking comfort, was as powerful and intimate as the firestorm of desire just moments ago.

"Look, the lion face is all dented."

Dev ran his fingers over the squashed nose. "I like it. Now it looks like a Persian, and hey, look on the bright side, if vampire hoards invade the school, we're totally prepared." He took the newly formed stake from her hand and made a stabbing motion through the air.

Her laughter was quickly becoming the highlight of his every waking moment. Knowing he was playing with fire, he couldn't resist one last kiss, a light brush of lips. "We're dating."

"So you said," her voice had dropped an octave at his caress. "Devlin—"

"Is the next sentence out of your mouth about to include the phrase 'special treatment'? Katherine, I already gave you my word." He drank in the sight of her. The single, blond curl that fell across her forehead. The sky-blue clarity of her eyes.

"That was before all the kissing."

"A promise is a promise, sweetheart, regardless of *all* the kissing."

"I don't want anyone here to know."

"Good luck with that. Jules already has dibs on matron of honour."

She put her hand on his cheek. "I'm serious."

"Any personal relationship we have wouldn't influence the admissions board. It won't affect your probation, or change the outcome of your final exam."

"You can't be sure of that."

"I can—" he broke off and kissed her forehead. "*Fine*, my stubborn little kitten. I won't say a word until you tell me to. When you do, I'll yell it from the rooftops for everyone to hear. Until then, I guess it's stolen kisses and secret girlfriends."

She glared at him in dramatic fashion. "*Now* you have girlfriends, plural? How many?"

Dev jerked his head towards the wardrobe. "At least four in there. They're keeping really quiet."

The intercom's beep was an unwelcome interruption. *"Boss, I'm not eavesdropping, I'm just reminding you to ring the accountant before your conference call at nine thirty."*

"And reality raises its ugly head once again." He forced himself from Katherine's side. "Promise me our dinner date is on."

"It's on. Where do you want me?"

By my side, forever.

"Back door at six?"

"Will do. Your tie is crooked," she tossed the last words over her shoulder.

"Whose fault is that?"

"I have no idea, it's not like we're *dating*." With a mischief filled wink, she was gone, leaving Dev with the sure and certain knowledge he was in love.

Katherine skipped down the stairs, rubbing at the ink mark on her shirt sleeve. She also had a coffee stain on her jeans. Devlin should take the blame for her day of clumsiness; memories of his kisses had dogged her through each and every class.

She found him just outside the back door, leaning against the wall, looking just as delectable as she remembered. "I'm not restaurant worthy."

"Good, I had something else planned."

"What?"

"If I tell you, it won't be a surprise."

"What if I don't like surprises?"

"Indulge me just this once, it'll be perfect."

Perfect.

An hour later, Katherine stretched out on the beach rug and plucked one last chip and a crispy piece of fish from the paper wrapped remnants between them. Waves lapped at the shore, glistening in the moonlight, and a fresh breeze was just enough to surround them in a sea scented tang of air without being too cold.

Devlin was sitting with one arm rested on his bent knee, his face half shadowed in profile, just as it had been at the piano. It was clear his mind was elsewhere.

"Okay, you win. This is perfect."

He turned at her words. "I'm glad. I come here when I want some peace. The ocean has its own specific rhythm and melody, don't you think? We'll do the posh restaurant next time if you like, with all the trimmings."

"I prefer this," Katherine hesitated before bringing up the subject that been bothering her all day. Phone calls, rushed interstate meetings, urgent demands from his accountant. Kat's worrying suspicion about what had been keeping Devlin so busy these last few weeks hadn't faded. "Can I ask you a question?"

"Yes, we're still dating."

"That's not the question." She rolled her eyes, and sat to gather up the food wrappings and put them to one side.

Just get it over with.

"Devlin, is Perdies in trouble?"

"I'm sorry, what?"

"Is Perdies in financial trouble? If it is, and you need someone to talk to, or confide in, please know I'm always here."

He scrambled to his knees in an elegant jumble of limbs, to cradle her face in his hands. "It's nothing like that."

"Are you sure? I mean... you've been running around like crazy for weeks, and zooming clear across the country every second day. You can trust me, you know you can, if you do need to talk about it. You shouldn't have to bear the weight of this on your own. I know what it's like to struggle. Businesses fail all the time and—" his fingers on her lips halted the torrent of words.

"Are you rushing to my aid like a knight-ess in shining armour?"

"I know what it's like to lose something precious, and knight-ess isn't a word."

"What did I ever do to deserve you?"

"I want to help. What can I do?"

"You can listen to me." He pulled her into his arms. "There *is* something going on, my keen-eyed little detective, and it's all hush-hush right now. But, it's not a financial problem. Quite the opposite. I've been approached by a syndicate of private investors with regards to taking Perdies nationwide."

Nothing he could have said could have stunned her more. "What? You mean, like a franchise?"

"I'm not a fan of that word, it sounds like I'm turning my music school into a fast-food chain, but, yes, that's the basic idea. This syndicate likes the concept of what we have here in Perth. The federation style building, the freeform classes, and they want to replicate it in other capital cities. I've been listening, and they've been talking, and talking, and *talking*, until my ears bleed and my brain turns to mush. I had to sign all sorts of non-disclosure agreements, and that's why I haven't said anything until now."

Kat's mind was spinning. He wasn't facing financial ruin. He was about to hit the big time. "Devlin, this is huge, this is *massive*."

"I know. It's also time consuming and right now that timing sucks. I'm zooming all over the country, as you so succinctly put it, at exactly the same time you're doing your probation. I don't want to be stuck in meetings in Sydney with people wooing me with truckloads of money and nationwide fame. I want to be at Perdies, with *you*, listening to your laughter echoing in the halls, hearing your beautiful singing voice while I'm working, all day every day. If it wasn't for the possibility of this franchise being such a brilliant idea, I'd tell them all to go to hell."

Katherine traced her fingers over the creases in his cotton shirt. Creases caused by her greedy, clutching fingers that very morning. The sincerity in his tone resonated with passion. The conflicting emotions his words stirred in her were a whirlwind, pushing and pulling her in different directions.

Okay, time to stop overthinking.

"Are you going to bring this level of romance to all our intimate encounters?"

That familiar chuckle made her toes curl. "Touché."

She scanned the deserted beach; they had the entire area to themselves. "Where's your phone?"

"At the office."

"Is Jules waiting somewhere behind a rock, getting ready to spring out at any second with an urgent message?"

"Bloody hell, I hope not."

She curled her fingers in his collar. “Well then, Mr. Perdie-Jones, soon to be billionaire businessman with a nationwide college named after him, we appear to be alone, and who knows when that’ll happen again. I suggest you kiss me, and keep kissing me.”

“Miss Grant, I like the way you think.”

The lapping waves were their melody; the moonlight was their guiding light, providing the perfect backdrop for a universe of kisses, and not a single interruption.

Chapter Six

My wardrobe misses you.

Kat bit back a grin as she read the latest message before replying.

Go away, I'm studying.

The response was instant.

The four other girlfriends in here are wondering where you are.

A couple of students frowned in her direction at the continuous vibration of her phone. Kat snatched it from the table with a murmured apology and hid it in her lap while she typed.

You're not in your wardrobe, you're in Melbourne.

Am I?

Wasn't he? Her fingers hovered over the keypad. In the last week he'd racked up more flight miles than she could keep track of, flitting from Sydney to Melbourne and Queensland and back again, checking out possible school sites and considering the proposals and options constantly being thrown at him. Theoretically, Devlin should be finishing up his latest meetings and on his way to Adelaide, before finally heading home tomorrow afternoon. Unless...

The class she was in wasn't one of hers, so she excused herself from the group, holding up her phone as an explanation, and headed downstairs. Or, she tried to, until someone grabbed her arm as she was passing the sun-room, yanking her inside.

"Devlin, you almost gave me heart failure." She punched him in the shoulder, even as that same heart leapt at the sight of him. "Why aren't you on a plane?"

"I told you, my wardrobe misses you." Each word was interspersed with kisses as his hungry fingers roamed over her hips, cradling her buttocks in his hands.

"Your wardrobe is one floor down."

"I figured you'd take thirty seconds to get there. I couldn't wait that long."

The sun-room had an extra feature today, an ornate, three panel Chinese screen partially obscuring the bay window seat. Kat marched him backwards. He went without objection, surrendering to her demands, until his knees hit the back of the seat and he went down with a bump. Kat followed, straddling his thighs. "Camouflage? Nice pre-planning."

"I was inspired."

"By us getting caught fooling around?"

"Precisely."

"My next class is in fifteen minutes. How long are you back for?"

"Half an hour. I need to be at the airport by four."

Kat pulled back to gawk at him. "Why on earth did you bother coming home? Couldn't you have got a direct flight?"

"Yes, but I needed to check on the cats. Mum's been doing all the cat sitting duty, but she's currently making sure my siblings don't run amok overseas, and there's only so many favours I can call in from my neighbours."

"At least you didn't stop off for half an hour just to kiss me."

"Katherine, my sweet, I'd fly half around the world for ten minutes just to kiss you. You're worth it." The words were spoken against her mouth.

How did he do that? Warm her soul with a few simple words. She'd known him for mere weeks and yet, after guarding her heart for so many years, he'd carved out a place in it. *Bad metaphor.*

Kat wriggled on his lap, eliciting a groan from him. He revelled in her touch every time. It made her bolder, more physically confident with him than she'd ever been in her previous, short-lived relationship. Although with Devlin, secret girlfriend and stolen kisses had meant exactly that. Kisses in his office. Kisses on the beach. At no time had he pressured her for anything more.

"Will you stop?" Devlin's fingers on her face brought her back to the present.

"Wriggling? I thought you liked it."

"You're thinking. Over thinking, I can see that little brain of yours working."

"Firstly, you cannot see my brain. Secondly, it isn't little. Thirdly, I was *thinking* I could keep an eye on your cats. It's about time I repaid you for all you've done."

"Katherine, our relationship doesn't have an invisible scale that needs balancing."

Yes, it does.

She fiddled with the buttons on his shirt. "I'd like to do it."

When he didn't respond, she lifted her eyes to find him staring at her. "What?"

"If I tell you, you'll either hit me or bolt."

"And you expect *not* to tell me after a statement like that?"

"I was just thinking."

"Over thinking?"

"Touché, little minx. You haven't been to my house."

"How short is your memory?"

"The doorstep doesn't count." He touched her cheek, a simple stroke of his fingertips. "I should cook for you after you've had a long day. Rub your shoulders when you've been studying too much."

There it was again. The ability to make her feel special, unique, *cherished.*

She had to swallow before answering. "You're traipsing across the country every second day. You barely have time to look after yourself, let alone me. Besides, we're new."

"Yeah, we are." That questing fingertip traced a journey to her throat. "You want to know something? I like us."

"Yeah, I like us too." If he said one more sweet thing, she'd embarrass herself and get emotional. Kat did *not* do emotional. She concentrated on that tantalising hint of hair visible below his first shirt button. "Is it a deal?"

"Fooling around in the sun-room for the next ten minutes? Definitely."

She had the satisfaction of seeing him wince as she yanked on his chest hair. "Looking after your cats."

"Absolutely. If I can wrap up these meetings in one hit, I'll be free, until I take the plunge on this deal. To sign on the dotted line or not. Then I'll be home for more than two days at a time. We can do this dating thing properly, instead of in short bursts. Why don't you stay?"

"Stay?" her gaze flew back up to meet his for the second time.

"Only if you want to."

"At your house?"

"That is where the cats are." That familiar mischief filled smile was back.

Kat tapped her fingers to her lips. "A free mini holiday at a stylish townhouse in one of the swankiest suburbs of Perth. One where the hot water doesn't run out after five minutes, and the stove actually works? I don't know Devlin, It's a tough choice."

The smile fell away. "You never told me your flat was that bad."

"I'm stubborn and independent, remember? Don't go into protector mode." She wrapped her arms around his neck, a distraction, and a comfort at the same time.

His sigh had a resigned edge. "You're definitely staying at my place."

"Bossy."

"Concerned. Big difference. And you'd be doing me a huge favour."

"In that case, I accept your invitation. Did we discuss how many wild parties I can have?" she batted her lashes at him in innocence.

"As many as you like, as long as you kiss me."

The sound of voices, and the opening of the sun-room door made Katherine jerk in alarm. She burrowed closer to Devlin, trying to hide as much of herself as possible behind the Chinese screen. He didn't appear the least bit alarmed as he tickled the bare skin on her stomach.

Stop that.

She mouthed the words at him, and was rewarded by a sensually impish smile.

"What about practicing in here, it's empty." The female voice was unfamiliar, as was the male reply.

"Nah, let's go outside instead, I'm dying for a smoke anyway."

They retreated as quickly as they'd arrived. At the click of the door, the breath Kat had been holding came out in a rush. "I thought we would get caught—why are you laughing?"

"You're worried about being seen? We're sitting in front of a window."

"On the first floor. No one can see us unless they're levitating."

"There you go again, bringing logic into the conversation."

"You want to keep talking? It's seven minutes to class time."

"In that case, I declare the conversation over." Winding his fingers into her hair, he hauled her closer for an open-mouthed kiss of such erotic passion, Kat's body temperature jumped up a full five degrees—or one hundred and fifty. If she could have gotten even closer, she would have, but it was impossible. They were joined, in a teasing, taunting simulation of lovemaking, her thighs clamped hard against his hips. His arousal was obvious, burning her sensitised flesh even through the two layers of fabric separating them. What would it be like to feel Devlin's hands all over her body, his lips tracing every inch of her naked skin?

"Katherine...Kat." His guttural words barely penetrated the sensual haze engulfing her. "Sweetheart, as much as I can't believe I'm saying this, our seven minutes are up."

Once again Devlin was the one to slam on the brakes while she was steaming ahead.

At least one of us is capable of coherent thought.

With the heat in her cheeks turning into a raging inferno, she tried to pull away. His arms tightened around her waist.

"Before you get up, you should know, I need to get certain things under control. Considering how we're currently positioned, I'm assuming you've noticed, and if you *haven't* noticed, please be aware my ego will be forever shattered."

"You mean that impressive bulge isn't your phone, or wallet, or a banana you'd saved for afternoon tea."

The fire in his eyes was a satisfying reward for her teasing. "You're trying to kill me."

"On the contrary, Mr Perdie, I'm trying to stimulate you. Remind me again, is it working?"

Devlin shifted positions on the loveseat with an obvious wince. "Were you a torturer in a previous life? Did I miss the words *Spanish Inquisition* on your resume?"

She scrambled to her feet and gave him a slow, sweeping look from head to toe. "I like you like this."

"Painfully aroused?"

She tapped a finger to her lips. "Deliciously dishevelled. It reminds me of the first time I met you."

Kat wasn't lying. The desire swirling in the room was almost enough to make her forget her next class. "How important is your next class?" He asked, reading her mind.

"Very important. I'm trying a duet with Tom."

"Is that a euphemism?"

She put an extra swing into her hips as she meandered past the screen. "Tom is *way* more interested in you than he is in me."

"That's a relief."

She paused by the doorway, "I'll tell him you said that."

Devlin pushed aside the Chinese screen, although she noticed he kept his lower body hidden. "These fifteen-minute hanky-panky sessions are torture, you know that, right?"

"You didn't have to come and see me."

"Yes, I did. Here," he tossed her a set of keys. "Enjoy my house, Katherine. I'll be thinking about you."

She caught them one handed. "I'm always thinking about you." She made her escape, before need overtook good sense and got them both arrested for public indecency.

Kat shouldered open the front door to Devlin's townhouse, and blocked the gap with her overnight bag, in case all his fur-kids staged a mass exodus. When no one rushed her, she gathered the bags of groceries and hauled everything inside. "Hello, puss, puss? Please don't tell me you've all run away. That'll take some explaining to your dad."

She'd only seen Devlin's beautiful home from the doorstep and was keen for the full tour. Call it natural curiosity, or professional interest, or outright nosiness.

Or all of the above.

His private life was a mystery to her. Apart from telling her he named Perdies after his mum, he barely spoke about his family, and Kat had been reluctant to bring the subject up in case there were underlying issues she knew nothing about. Perhaps his home would give her some clues. As she suspected, the interior was stunning, a gorgeous mix of sleek, modern furniture with eclectic elements of old-world charm. A piano sat front and centre in the main living space. Two acoustic guitars were leaning against the wall, along with framed pieces that looked like vintage sheet music. A long modular sofa faced a sleek looking

TV and built in cabinets housed a state-of-the-art hi-fi system. It didn't surprise her that Devlin's home would be geared towards sound. Interestingly, there were no family photos. In fact, all the walls, shelves, and flat surfaces were bare of any ornamentation. Kat put her phone and handbag on the marble coffee table with an almost guilty trepidation, hoping she wasn't breaking some sort of minimalist rule.

"Don't be an idiot. He said to make myself at home, didn't he? Great, now I'm talking to myself. Puss, puss. C'mon, cats where are you hiding?"

Devlin's kitchen had her rubbing her hands together in glee at the mere *thought* of cooking there. She'd been reduced to a single, partially working hot plate for the last six months and a stove that could only be described as temperamental. Her modest little flat was a homage to 1970's in both décor and electrics.

Visions of perfect roasts and exotic stir-fries were shattered by a loud crash from somewhere inside the house. Kat snatched up the first weapon she could find, a metal spatula, and tiptoed back along the corridor. Her racing heart slowed when she saw her handbag and its contents spread out on the polished floorboards. Its former position on the coffee table had been taken by an indignant looking cat. "Hello, Evita. I'm beginning to see why all Devlin's surfaces are bare. Hold on, wait—" Her phone suffered the same fate as the bag, via a quick flick of a paw. Kat waved the spatula in the cat's direction. The threat was less than successful. Evita gave her a long, slow blink and washed her face in languid strokes.

A brush against her ankles resulting in another heart-rending shock until Kat saw a second cat winding in and out of her feet.

"Hello, Othello. Do you know how I know your name? Because Devlin sent me identification photos. I have no clue about his family, but I know all his pets' names. Why do I have the feeling you lot have your dad wrapped around your little fingers... or paws in this case. I've never had a cat, so don't expect me to be as much of a pushover." Kat picked up the purring Othello, who tucked his head under her chin and snuggled closer. *Dammit.* Kat's heart melted on the spot.

Carmen, the third member of the feline trio, dashed under her feet as she walked back to the kitchen with Othello still in her arms, almost sending her sprawling. "Bloody hell, you lot are a death trap. I'm amazing Devlin has survived this long."

When all three cats were munching on biscuits, from *personalised* bowls that made Kat grin, she continued her tour of the house. The spacious townhouse had three bedrooms. Two were beautifully furnished, with the beds made up ready for guests, the third was more of a storage room with framed artwork and photos stacked in piles against the walls. Kat sniffed, catching the faint scent of fresh paint. The walls were pristine, without a mark or a smudge, or a picture hook. It looked like Devlin had been doing some renovations. She resisted the urge to look through the stacked frames and made her way back to the largest of the bedrooms, standing just outside the door. *This* room was Devlin's. It wasn't just the bold, solid colours of the décor, or the jacket tossed over a chair. The room *felt* like him. Kat drew in a deep slow breath, catching the faintest hint of that subtle fragrance she associated with him even through the lingering paint smell. Could she sleep here? *Should* she sleep here? The thought of sharing the same sheets he'd used sent a shiver of arousal along her body. Something caught her eye, sitting on a high shelf of the built-in bookcase. Her heart sank as she recognised the broken cane stored in a place even the cats couldn't reach. He'd brushed off the loss as unimportant. That was clearly untrue. The cane was part of Perdies' history, and now it was a smashed remnant. She pulled the two pieces down, standing on tiptoes to reach. Maybe it could be repaired? No, she could see in an instant, the wood was splintered in angry jagged lines, destroying the strength and integrity of the object. Kat nibbled on her lip, she couldn't repair, but maybe she could replace? Taking the two pieces back downstairs she snapped some photos, and hit the internet. Two hours later, with quotes and websites and scribbled information covering her trusty Hello Kitty notebook, and sleeping cats all around her, Kat leaned back in the chair and stretched out the kinks in her spine. "I think this might work, puss-cats. I think this might just work."

Her sense of satisfaction was marred by a loud unladylike rumble from her stomach. With a grin of pure anticipation, Kat made a beeline for Devlin's kitchen.

The shrill ringing of a phone woke her in the early hours. Kat stretched out a hand towards the noise, fumbling in the dark and the unfamiliar surroundings. "Hello?"

"Did I wake you?"

The sound of Devlin's voice was welcome, even in her half-awake state. "It's fine, don't worry about it." Kat tried to move her legs, confused by the weight holding them down. She flicked on the bedside lamp, not altogether surprised to see three cats covering her lower body like a furry blanket. "How did the last lot of meetings go?"

"Well, I think. We toured several buildings. One is too modern, the other is a renovation nightmare. The third might work. Would you like to see?"

He'd been doing this for weeks, sending her pictures of federation buildings, asking for her opinion. "I'd love to."

She held the phone out when it beeped, rubbing the sleep from her eyes, trying to focus on the small image. "It looks like our Perdies."

"I know. It's a great location too." He gave her a quick rundown on the specs, and the work needed to turn the beautiful building into a music school. Kat snuggled under the covers to listen. The enthusiasm in his voice was contagious, enticing.

"Where are you?" the change of subject took her off guard.

"In bed. Where else would I be at five in the morning?"

"Which room?" his voice had dropped a full octave.

"Guess." She could do the low-sexy-voice-thing too.

His indrawn breath made her grin. "Christ, Katherine, you're in my bed, aren't you?"

"Maybe, but I have a confession to make," she lowered her voice to a sultry whisper, "I'm not alone."

Devlin burst out laughing—so much for rousing his jealous passion— "I should have warned you to close the door. How many cats are on there with you?"

"Three, although it feels like ten. How much do they weigh, for God's sake?"

"The girls are the heavy ones. Othello is a lightweight. I'm sorry, sweetheart, are they disturbing you?"

Not as much as his voice down the line when she was sprawled naked on his sheets.

"What are you wearing?" Devlin's tone had dropped back to sex on a stick, and, sheesh, was he a mind reader?

"Guess."

This time, his intake of breath was a hiss of sound. "Katherine, are you nude in my bed?"

"What if I was?"

"I'd ask if I could join you."

"The answer would be yes."

"In that case, I only have one more question."

"What's that?"

"How do you feel about kissing me goodnight."

Wait, what? Kat bolted upright as Devlin's voice echoed loud in the room, *not* the phone.

"By the way," his disembodied voice continued, "did I mention I've had an intercom installed?"

Cats scattered in every direction, meowing in complaint as she leapt from the bed and jammed her arms through her robe, cursing as the silky material resisted her efforts. She managed some semblance of modesty by the time she made it to the bottom stair and flung open the door.

"I'm a tiger, I'm a tiger." Dev stood on the other side, leaning against the jam. A grin finished his impromptu serenade as he released the intercom button.

"You're here." The words were blurted out in a rush. Wow, talk about stating the obvious.

"I am."

"When? How?" *Now I'm just stringing words together.*

Devlin held three fingers up. "Ten minutes ago, and a plane, followed by a cab."

"You're not due back until at least tomorrow."

"I know. Listen. I was going to Mum's place being as it's empty, but I gave the taxi driver this address. I just wanted to check, to see if you were okay. I don't have to come in—"

Kat silenced his words with a kiss, throwing her arms around him, and holding on as if her life depended on it, until they were both gasping for air. "You're not going anywhere."

"Okay." His voice was agreeably husky.

Releasing her limpet like grip on his body, she turned and started up the stairs, throwing him a look over her shoulder. "I'll race you to the bedroom, Mr. Perdie-Jones."

"You don't have to tell me twice—umph." Not for the first time since she'd known him, his last word ended on a grunt. Not for the first time, Kat turned back to see him sprawled on the ground. An indignant looking Carmen stood mere inches away, licking at a paw.

"Is it too much to ask that we have *one* day where I get to be the hero instead of the court jester?" Devlin's voice was so annoyed, so utterly resigned, Kat fought back laughter.

"I like you like this."

"Looking like a complete idiot?"

Kat tilted her head to one side. "I prefer to think of it as worshipping at my feet." She drew her fingers through the belt of the robe, pulling it free. "Are you coming? Or are you just going to lay there."

"Katherine, two broken legs couldn't keep me on this floor." To prove his point, he jumped up. She evaded his hands by sprinting up the stairs, their joint laughter echoing off the walls.

He caught her as she reached his bed, tumbling her back onto it. The silky robe disappeared in seconds.

His clothes took longer, but only just. Leather shoes hit the ground with a thud. She grabbed at his shirt, her eager fingers doing irreparable damage to the fiddly button holes. "Can I suggest T-shirts as a clothing option?"

"I'll burn my entire wardrobe tomorrow." He solved the button problem by hauling the shirt over his head, tossing it aside while she tackled his trousers, loving the groan torn from his lips when her fingers grazed him. Within moments there was nothing between them. A whirlwind of emotion clogged her throat as she reached for him, relishing the glorious sensation of skin-to-skin contact.

"Tell me if I'm rushing you." Even now his thoughts were only for her.

She nipped his ear in response, humming a tune against his skin, empowered by the way his body jerked in response. "Seducing me with your voice is not playing fair."

"I'm not in a fair playing mood."

They chased the approaching dawn in fevered haste. Lost in sensation. Lost in passion. Lost in each other.

Touches became bolder. Breath became harsher. The entire world could have blinked out of existence and Kat wouldn't have noticed. At this moment, her world was right here, caught in the tangled sheets as pleasure drove her higher, ending in a blinding flash of release to rival the most exquisite music ever created.

One thought echoed in her desire-soaked mind.

I'm home.

Chapter Seven

When Kat tiptoed into the bedroom carrying a glass of orange juice, she had a momentary qualm about morning after awkwardness. The thought was swept away when she saw Othello curled up on the pillow next to Devlin's head.

Devlin lifted those sooty lashes at her chuckle. He stretched in the sunlight streaming through the window, causing the low-slung sheet to play peek-a-boo with his naked lower body. "What?" his voice was deep with sleep and spent passion.

"You're wearing your cat as a hat."

"Isn't that a Dr Seuss book?" He propped himself up on one elbow and took the glass from her hand, downing its contents in seconds and giving her a sweeping look from head to toe at the same time. "Speaking of wearing things. You appear to have commandeered my shirt."

Kat forced the blush from her cheeks. "I'm repurposing it. The button holes are torn."

"It wasn't a complaint, my sweet. What time is it?"

"Almost ten. I have a class in an hour."

"You should have woken me earlier."

"No way. Have you *seen* how you look lately? You're running on fumes and sheer determination." Kat knelt on the bed beside him. "Are you going to tell me why you took an impromptu red-eye and ended up on your doorstep at five in the morning? Didn't you trust me with your cats?"

"I trust you with my life, Katherine. I flew home early because I'd made a decision." Devlin took a deep breath and released it. "I'm going ahead with the deal, with one change. I want controlling rights to the name, and all the major decisions."

"That sounds like more work for you."

"It is, but my gut is telling me it's the right thing to do. It will either work and be a huge success, or it'll fail miserably and you'll end up as my only student."

Kat brushed a kiss across his lips. "I'd be proud to be your only student. You could have told me this over the phone."

He wrapped his hand around the back of her neck, pulling her closer. "You're important to me. I wanted to tell you in person, and warn you I haven't finished continent hopping yet."

She allowed him to draw her down to the rumbled bed. "In other words, you're still looking for a free cat sitter."

"Stay." The word was breathed onto her neck in a rush of warm air. "Stay for you, and for us. Stay, so I know I can at least see you whenever my feet touch solid ground. Stay, so I can kiss your sweet mouth, and revel in the touch of your skin... and, yes, I *really* need a cat sitter."

Laughter and heat. She'd always associated that combination with Devlin. The stubble on his chin was an erotic rasping, almost making her forget about the voice tuition she had booked in fifty-five minutes, *almost*. Kat pushed aside sensual imaginings of their bodies locked together. "I'll stay, and I want the rest of the story, every single detail, but now I have to go."

"Right now?"

"Right now."

"Right, *right* now?" His fingers traced a path along the curve of her hip.

"Devlin!"

"Katherine." If his name on her lips was a laughter filled demand, hers on his was a beguiling entreaty, a coaxing, cajoling plea she was powerless to resist.

Why am I even trying?

Kat curled her leg over his. "If I'm late for class, I'm blaming you."

"I accept full responsibility."

Katherine.

"Katherine? Kat?" Bill's questioning tone broke through her highly charged erotic memory. Devlin was a bad influence on her attention span. "I asked if you agreed with my suggestion, to leave the key change until the last chorus and hold the final note a moment longer."

"It's perfect. It changes the overall impact, and creates heaps more emotion, thanks Bill."

"It's what they pay me for. Same time next week? That will be our second to last tuition before the big day. How are you feeling about it?" Bill gathered up his music sheets, stuffing them into his well-worn briefcase.

"Excited. Terrified. Overwhelmed."

"All perfectly natural emotions. You'll do well, Kat, if anyone deserves a full placement at Perdies, it's you." With those comforting words, he left, for his next coaching session.

The teachers were rushing around like crazy. All the probationary students were trying to cram in as many one-on-one tuitions as they could manage before the final exam.

Jules passed Kat on the stairs brandishing a large envelope. "This came by courier. Could you give it to Dev for me?"

Kat halted mid step. "Me? Why would I—I mean, can't you courier it to his house?"

"Didn't he con you into cat sitting? Something about the stove not working at your place? That's what Dev told me." The innocence in Jules' tone was ruined by the mischievous expression on her face.

"Oh, right. Yes, yes, that's right, I am."

"Good. Make sure he reads it before the two of you get distracted by other things." Jules continued her way, leaving Kat with red cheeks.

Ava almost stumbled through a door on her left, overbalanced as usual by her cello. Kat grabbed the heavy instrument as Ava shoved a wayward swatch of hair off her forehead with a sigh. "I'm going to put in a class suggestion to the big boss. All string lessons from now on should be conducted on the ground floor only."

"You should. The students mean everything to Dev—Mr Perdie."

"I'm going to watch Tom practice with the seniors, you coming?"

"Sure."

Devlin sent her a message later that afternoon.

"Text me when you're coming home. I'll cook dinner."

It was immediately followed by a second message.

"If you don't like lamb, text me now."

Kat sprang through the day with lightness in her heart.

Kat rinsed the last of the plates and stacked them in the dishwasher, revelling in the marvels of a modern kitchen.

"You didn't need to do that." Devlin called from the living room.

"Yes, I did. It's only fair, you cooked." She wiped down the granite benchtop and gave the sparkling clean surfaces one last satisfied look before joining him, only to chuckle when she saw the tribe of cats curled up around him on the sofa.

"Sorry," he lifted Othello from his usual spot tucked into his neck.

"Leave him, I'm aware of my pecking order status in the household when daddy's home." Kat brushed a kiss over his mouth, scratched Othello's ear and retreated to the comfortable leather chair opposite.

"They're used to having me all to themselves."

"So, I see," Kat picked up the Edith Piaf biography, but discarded it, more interested in Devlin's life than her favourite singer. "How did you end up as the world's cutest crazy cat man? Did you get them all as kittens?"

He grinned at her wink. "Only Othello here. I've had him since I was nine." Devlin tickled the purring cat under the chin. "He loves his cuddles, in this same spot, snuggled against my chest. And he loves the sunshine, he has his favourite spot in the garden, he'll sit there for hours. Do I sound like an idiot? A genuine crazy cat man?"

"Maybe. Maybe I *like* crazy cat men."

He shifted Othello to one side, next to the others. The ousted puss grunted, but settled down and went back to sleep. "Evita and Carmen came from the cat haven four years ago. They'd been left in a box outside when they were around six months old and had clearly bonded. It was a case of buy one get one free. They're inseparable, in case you hadn't noticed."

"I had noticed."

"Carmen had some early health issues, problems with her lungs, but she's fine now, and I suspect my vet has a lovely holiday home in Italy."

Kat grinned at the pained look on his face. "And there you have it, my cat history in all its glorious detail." He held out his hand.

Kat slipped her fingers into his. "Where are we going?"

"To the mirror."

"Is this a kink thing?"

A bark of laughter escaped him. "Do not put that idea into my head, young lady, this is purely professional."

She allowed him to tug her upstairs into one of the spare bedrooms with a full-length mirror in the corner. He positioned her front and centre, and stood behind her. "What song have you chosen for your final audition?"

"You *know* I can't tell you that."

"Just a hint, up-tempo? Slow ballad? 60's pop song?"

"Does the phrase 'special treatment' ring any bells?"

"I told you this is strictly professional. I'm about to give you a lesson in breathing and distractions. And before you say anything, I've done the same thing for other students over the years."

Kat threw him a look, and finally relented. “Up-tempo ballad, that’s all you’re getting.”

“Good. Now, look at yourself in the mirror, keep your focus tight, and concentrate on your breathing. I want you to sing, *not* the audition song, obviously, just something slow, something you’re comfortable with.”

Kat ran her vast repertoire through her mind and decided on a classic. Olivia Newton John's *Hopelessly Devoted To You*. She barely got through the first line before Devlin clapped his hands next to her ear, the sudden noise turning the melodic note into a strident squeak.

He grinned at her in the mirror. “Distractions.”

She elbowed him backwards in the ribs. “I didn’t realise the judges were going to be setting traps.”

“They’re not. This is just an exercise. When we’re nervous, every sound and movement is magnified. It’s the body’s natural fight or flight reaction.” He ran his thumbs along her jaw “You’ll tense up here, and here,” his hand moved to her throat. “Your breathing will change and all those things will directly affect your voice.”

“I’ve sung in public before.”

"Yes, and that's a good thing, but the mind is a strange creature. It will keep reminding you how important this audition is, how you *can't* mess it up, and hey presto, your body reacts to that stress and your voice wavers and fails."

"If such a reaction is visceral, how do I stop it?"

"Don't try. This is energy, an adrenal response. Don't fight it, channel it into the song. The idea is to block everything out except the sound of your own voice and the feel of your breath. Try again."

"No clapping."

"You have my word."

With a wry look at his hands in plain view on her shoulders, she started over. This time she got to the chorus before he kissed the side of her neck. Her breath exited in a rush, yanking the power from the long note she was trying to hold.

"Distractions." The word was murmured against her skin.

"Are you *sure* this is an official exercise?"

"Absolutely."

"And you've done this with how many other students?"

The murmur morphed into a chuckle, a purr of vibration sending an echo throughout her body. "My distraction techniques are different with you."

"I'm glad to hear it."

"Jealous?"

"Don't be ridiculous. I just don't want to have to report you."

"There's my true romantic." Devlin nipped her earlobe, making her jump.

On the song's third attempt, he slipped a button of her cotton shirt free and ran his fingers along her abdomen. Kat held her focus, and the high note, mentally punching the air when it rang true and clean, even as her eyes were drawn to the movement of his fingers across her skin. Another button slipped free, and another until the shirt was fully open. She sang as his exploratory touch grazed the underside of her breast. Sang as he laid kisses on the back of her neck and moved closer until his body was in full contact with hers. With his words running through her mind like a mantra, she channelled all her excess tension and the adrenalin borne rush of desire, into her voice, into the song.

It almost worked, until he tickled her side, ruining the very last note. Her eyes flew to his in the mirror. "Oh, come on, that's not fair."

His laughter was low and sexy. His expression was a potent mixture of mischief, pride, and desire. "Let's go again, from the beginning."

She lasted a whole verse and half the chorus, her breath finally hitched when he unfastened her front fastening bra and nudged the two sides apart, until they clung to her nipples. She focussed on the erotic images playing out in real time in front of her. His tanned hands were dark against her pale skin, and every light, exploratory touch of his fingers, was an exquisite torture.

"Well done." The compliment was a whisper against her ear. "Keep going."

When he moved his hands lower, and traced the waistband of her yoga pants, Kat's heartbeat sped up. She could feel it in her throat, impacting the rhythm of her voice.

She closed her eyes to concentrate and Devlin nipped her on the neck. "That's cheating. Watching is part of the exercise."

She broke from the song to give him a wry look in the mirror. "Really?"

"Really and truly."

She began again from the top, and kept singing even when Devlin's hands slid lower, sneaking beyond the waistband to touch her aching flesh. Kat fought back the flush of heat burning her face even as his wordless hum caressing her skin told her he approved of the lack of underwear.

The scorching blush was nothing now, compared to the heat building in her body. Devlin's questing fingers swept between her folds, moving back and forth, keeping in time with the melody of the song.

Has anything ever been so erotic as being stirred to release to the sound of your own voice?

That became her focus, the rhythmic movement of his fingers as he stroked her, pushing her past the point of no return. She blinked as her pupils dilated, blurring the sensual image, and still she sang, concentrating on each breath, each note. A tightening of her abdominal muscles threatened to derail her performance and she added that to her focus, working with it, using the tension, feeding on it.

She was close… so close. A tingling sensation started in her toes and worked slowly upwards, bringing a promise in its wake. Two more lines, one more line, one last note. The final power chord burst from her lips as the climax took hold, crashing her synapses, rendering her powerless to *everything* except sensation.

"Oh, dear God." Kat sagged against him, held up only by Devlin's hand on her waist and the other still pressed against her pulsating flesh.

His low laughter was an added sensual pleasure. "I don't remember that line, are you improvising, my sweet?"

"I can't believe I did that."

"Had an orgasm? Or hit that last "F" at exactly the same time."

"Both." Kat released a shuddering breath. "I've never watched myself before."

"Next time, we'll do it naked."

The mere thought of that was enough to send a second wave of pulses deep inside her core as he slowly removed his hand from her. "Speaking of naked."

"Hmm?" His look was pure innocence.

"I need you to remove every scrap of clothing right now."

"Yours or mine."

"Both." She spun in his embrace and draped her arms around his neck. "It's been two seconds. Why are you still dressed?"

"Your wish is my command."

Clothes flew in all directions, mostly under Devlin's direction. Kat's pleasure-soaked brain could barely function, let alone manage something as complex as zips and buttons.

She pulled him to the carpet, straddling his hips, needy and desperate. He groaned as she pushed down, and curled his hands around her hips as he sank home with one strong thrust.

Kat threw her head back with a cry, drowning in pleasure.

"Sing for me sweet Katherine, never stop."

She did, the power of it sweeping them both away.

"Katherine?"

She bolted upright in her chair like a guilty ten-year-old. "What? Sorry?" God, if she didn't get a black mark for inattention for her constant day dreaming, it would be a miracle.

Her classmates sniggered, and the teacher gave her a sympathetic look. "It's natural to be distracted the day before the exam. Try not to worry about it. Listen up, everyone. We're almost done. Here's a summary of what you need to know. *Please* write this down, or at least commit it to memory. The first hour will consist of an interview. *All* your teachers, including me, will have submitted reports on your probationary period. The committee will want to ask questions, be sure you answer truthfully, and in full. Then comes the moment of truth, your live solo. Choose your music carefully, this decision is important to your future. Okay, that's all from me. If you'll head to the downstairs meeting room, Mr Perdie will give you the final rundown on tomorrow's big day. Good luck everyone."

Kat's class, along with the rest of the students made their way to the lower level and took their seats. The excited gathering was a call back to her very first day at Perdies. A palpable energy permeated the room, all focused on the man who strode to the podium set up at the front.

Kat heard murmured voices circling her as a melodic wave. One phrase stood out from the rest.

No cane.

Ava bent to whisper. "He doesn't look crippled to me."

Kat hid her smile by ducking her head. "I think that was a rumour."

Tom's stage whisper in her other ear was loud enough to be heard in the next suburb. "Sheesh, that's a great arse. I bet he's great in the sack."

"Tom." Kat elbowed him in the ribs, forcing the burning heat from her cheeks by sheer will power.

Devlin cleared his throat and the room fell into instant silence.

"Good morning, everyone. Well, here we are on the last official day of your probation. A few short weeks ago you all walked through that door with passion and determination in your hearts. I hope in *my* heart that Perdies has given you the skills to nurture that passion, regardless of your exam results tomorrow. Tomorrow may be your last day with us, but if your probation ends without a full placement, please remember it does not signal the end of your talent. Persistence is key. You've chosen a tough dream to follow, and people will try to knock you down, talk you into doing something sensible," Devlin's eyes caught hers for a moment. "The choices have to be yours, not theirs. If you end up singing in a café once a week on a Sunday, or if you steam full speed ahead, searching for that elusive contract that will bring your music to the whole world, do it for yourself, because you *need* to, because your life would be incomplete without at least trying to reach for the stars. Whatever you choose, let it bring you joy and happiness as your music has brought joy and happiness into my school." He let his words sink in, and at that moment you could have heard a pin drop in the spacious room.

"Now, onto some necessary, but boring details. Your teachers will have told you about the exam. I need to reiterate that punctuality is the most vital thing you need to remember. If you miss your appointed time, you will *not* have a second chance. A broken alarm clock? A traffic jam? None of these excuses will cut it. It's because of this that Perdies will be open to all probationary students from six tomorrow morning. All full-time students will have the day off, the entire school is yours. Breakfast and lunch buffets will be set up in different rooms, including smoothie stations, pop up coffee shops and even a bar. The last two items are only available for students *after* their exams. The judges have no desire to see you jittery or drunk." He grinned when a series of good-natured groans echoed around them. "There will also be massage stations and meditation sessions throughout the day. Once your evaluation is complete, you may stay as long as you like providing you do not share details of the questions to those students still waiting. If all of that is clear, can I get a 'Hell Yeah'?" a momentary pause followed his request, and few brave students responded in murmured tones.

Devlin put his hands on his hips. "Excuse me, I don't think I made myself clear. You've finished your probation. Tomorrow, your new life begins. Now, can I get a 'Hell Yeah'?"

"Hell Yeah"

The wall of sound was so deafening, Kat clamped her hands over her ears. The impromptu battle cry was followed by genuine laughter as the tension in the room dissipated, replaced by excitable chatter.

Devlin caught her gaze for a second time, giving her an almost imperceptible wink. Kat rolled her eyes, and was rewarded by one of his bright smiles.

As they filed from the room, Kat's phone beeped a message *"First floor kitchen."*

Excusing herself from the masses, she headed there to see a travel cup sitting on the counter steaming with aromatic flavours.

Tea

Kat cradled it in her hands, unable to wipe the smile from her face. Perdies' owner didn't control her life or influence her choices. No, he just made her tea.

A second message followed the first. *"Narnia"*

Jules was absent from her desk, giving Kat an unobserved passage into Devlin's office. She eased open the wardrobe door and yelped in surprise when he tugged her inside.

She swatted him with her free hand, eyes trying to adjust to the dark interior. "Sheesh, are you trying to give me a heart attack? And I almost drowned you in hot tea."

"That's the reason for the travel cup, my sweet. Besides, I'll suffer third degree burns if it means having you in my arms." Her attempted reply was cut off by his mouth, and that was fine, she couldn't think of an appropriate response anyway.

"Hi." He stroked a line down her cheek several enjoyable kisses later. "I need to go to Adelaide."

Cue the mood breaker. "When? Why? I thought all the franchise stuff was done and dusted"

"Why? One idiotic missing signature on one idiotic piece of paper. When? As soon as I leave this wardrobe."

"Devlin, that's crazy. You need some downtime and sleep before you have a major physical burnout. Can't they fax it or courier it or something?"

"Trust me, I went through every option. Flying over is the quickest way. I'll have to catch the redeye back, which means returning home at some ungodly hour. The official landing time is two fifty-five am. I just wanted to let you know. I'll creep in and crash in the spare room."

"I have a better idea, I'll sleep at my place tonight."

Even in the darkness she could see the frown on his face. "I don't want that."

She ran her thumb over his lips. "Let's be logical. I'll be here at six tomorrow morning. I'll get a better night's sleep if it's not interrupted, no offense."

"None taken, I hate it when you're logical." He kissed her fingers.

"I'll feed the cats and have an early night. Are you coming here tomorrow?"

"I wouldn't miss it for the world."

"Because that's what you always do every year? Not because it's *my* assessment day?"

His laughter was a balm to her senses. "Ask Jules if you don't believe me. I'll stay in my office, you don't have to worry about me hovering."

"Promise you'll message me when you get home at three-something tomorrow morning."

"I will as long as you only turn your phone on when you get up."

"I will. Promise me you won't get here at six. The first evaluation isn't until nine anyway."

"Is that a hint, Katherine? Is that when your allotted time is?"

"You know I'm not telling you that, right?"

"You could give me a broad hint, morning? Afternoon?"

"Nope, not gonna happen. I don't want you thinking of me when I'm singing. And don't call me tomorrow."

That sexy chuckle of his could become addictive. "You *do* know I think about you all the time, right? Fine, I won't call as long as you promise *me,* you'll come here to my office after your exam, whenever it is, and let me know how it went?"

"Hmm… I don't know about that. I hear there's a smoothie station *and* a pop-up bar, I might be too busy."

"Cheeky minx." He nipped her earlobe.

Kat draped her arms around his neck. "Of course, I'll come and see you, crazy cat man."

"Is that my official title now?"

"If the cap fits…"

"Or the cat." He smiled against her mouth, and stole several more kisses.

Kat broke free with reluctance. "Shouldn't you be going?"

"I'd rather be coming, but I'm hoping we can rectify that later."

"Devlin!"

"Katherine." His lips captured again.

I could so easily fall in love with you, Devlin Sebastian Perdie-Jones.

Chapter Eight

THE UNEXPECTED SOLITARY END to the day gave Kat a chance to pick up her special order. The craftsman smiled as he handed it over. “Is it a gift?”

“Yes.” Kat examined the cane. She hadn’t wanted to replicate the original; instead, she’d created her own version and added some practical elements. The stick itself was brass, and folded into three pieces for air travel. The carved cat’s head was wooden, a beautiful rich Jarrah. She traced the feline features with her fingers. “It’s beautiful.”

"You gave me excellent instructions, and it was a pleasure to make. I'm guessing it's for someone pretty special."

A bloom of heat warmed her cheeks as she gave him a shy look. "Yeah, he is."

Her apartment was stale and dark when she shoved open the warped door as night was falling. Kat stood for a moment, taking in her meagre possessions and the familiar, practical furniture. The place no longer seemed like home. Had it ever truly been her home?

The simple answer was no.

She shook off her melancholy mood. What Devlin had said in his final speech ran true. Tomorrow was the start of a new life, whatever the outcome of her exam.

Would that life include Devlin? Did she want it to?

The simple answer was yes.

Despite all her good intentions, butterflies in her stomach kept her from sleeping as soundly as she'd hoped. Kat kept her eye on the clock over an early morning coffee, wanting to give herself extra time in case of traffic jams, nuclear explosions, the zombie apocalypse, or anything else the universe threw at her. She ran her music choice through her mind, humming as she washed the mug. After weeks of agonising, she'd chosen an up-tempo balled from one of Tina Arena's popular French albums. Singing in another language was risky, but the song was a personal favourite, and at least the committee wouldn't have heard it a hundred times before.

I hope.

Her phone beeped the moment she switched it on with a message from Devlin and a photo, both sent at four-fifteen in the morning. Three disgruntled, sleepy looking cats were staring at the camera. A hand written note propped between them said, *break a leg.*

The message was punctuated with a love heart emoji.

Kat touched the tiny symbol, pushing aside the joy it created in her own heart.

Perdies was bustling with excitement when she arrived at exactly six. Kat juggled her bag and the change of clothes in her arms. After an age of undecided time wasting, which resulted in her entire wardrobe being consigned to the bed in piles, she'd finally chosen a simple black jersey dress and mid height heels. But, not wanting to get too dressed up so early in the morning, she'd opted for an old but comfy jeans, T-shirt and sneakers combo to pass away the morning hours. It appeared everyone else had the same idea. She spied an already bulging portable clothing rack in the corner of the room and added her hanger to the crowded mix. Devlin hadn't exaggerated when he said 'breakfast buffet'. Three chefs working at long trestle tables were flipping pancakes and cooking omelettes with enthusiasm and obvious talent. Giant platters of fresh fruit and heavenly smelling pastries were piled high in every corner. "Wow."

"I know, right?" Tom spoke around a mouthful of egg. "Check out the smoothie station next door, it's amazing. Ava headed straight for the massage centre. I told her to take it easy. She won't be able to play the cello if her arms are relaxed noodles."

"What time's your evaluation?"

"Eleven thirty. You?"

"Two thirty."

"Ava's must be just before you. How are you feeling?"

"Nervous. Excited."

"Yep, that about sums it up."

Jules stepped into the room, waving her clip board like a weapon. "Okay, you lot, this is your friendly reminder to be downstairs at least fifteen minutes before your allotted time. Afterwards you can go home, or head to the bar. That's where you'll find me." With those final words, she turned on her heel and left them.

Tom leant close to Kat and whispered, "Do you think she even enjoys working here?"

Kat grinned at him. "I've often wondered that myself."

A light but healthy breakfast, two cups of fresh juice, and several conversations with other excited students made the morning fly by. She gave Tom a long hug before his time slot which he gave back with enough force to push the air from her lungs. He didn't return afterwards and she spied him outside in the bar area with the increasing crowd of post-exam people, sculling what looked like a large brandy. Kat's nerves kicked in. She put a hand to her fluttering stomach, and took several deep breaths. A quick check of her phone confirmed no messages. Devlin would still be asleep, hopefully. He'd promised not to call and she refused to backtrack on her own instructions and ring him, no matter how much she wanted to hear his voice.

Instead, she headed upstairs to the library, empty as usual, and sat on the floor, surrounded by books, stretching out her neck and shoulder muscles and doing some vocal exercises.

At one thirty she headed to her car to retrieve Devlin's gift and made her way to the main entrance area, where chairs had been set up along the corridor, just as they had on her very first day at Perdies. Ava's cello was propped against the wall outside one of the doors. Kat sent her friend some good vibes. Devlin's office door was closed. Jules was sitting at her desk tapping on her keyboard.

Kat approached and lowered her voice. "Can I ask you a favour?"

She looked up. "You want me to hack the computer and rig today's exam results? I'm not usually up for bribery, but tell me what you're offering and I'll let you know."

Her acerbic tone made Kat smile. "That's *not* what I'm asking. Could you hold on to this for me while I'm having my assessment?" Kat lifted the gift bag in her hand. "It's for Devlin."

“Sure, if you want, but he’s not here.”

Kat hesitated with the bag still raised in mid-air. “Is he out getting lunch?”

“He hasn’t been here all day, because of the cat thing.”

“Cat thing? What cat thing?” Kat’s stomach dropped as she fumbled for her phone. The message screen was blank. “Is one of them sick? Has he called the vet?”

“It’s too late for that, apparently.”

Pain speared through Kat’s chest.

Too late for the vet.

“Kat, where are you going? You can’t leave.”

Jules words barely registered. Kat didn’t answer. She couldn’t speak, or even breathe. She flew along the corridor, weaving past students coming the other way. One of them said something, she didn’t hear what. All her focus was on one thing and one thing only.

Getting to Devlin.

Snippets of conversations and memories ran through her mind like a loop. Evita and her antibiotics. Carmen and her lung problems.

Please let Jules be wrong, please let it all be a mistake.

The traffic was light and still she ground her teeth at every red signal, every slow-moving car. When she reached the stylish townhouse, she parked haphazardly and bolted up the pathway.

"Devlin?" The door was ajar, and gave under her hand. "Devlin?"

The first thing she saw was Evita sitting on the kitchen counter washing her paws. Carmen was next to her, sleeping.

That left only one option. *No, no, no, not Othello.*

Devlin stood by the glass patio doors, arms limp by his side. His entire body language radiating grief and pain. Reaching him in seconds, she wrapped her arms around him from behind.

He turned in her embrace, "Katherine?"

Her worst suspicions were confirmed by the anguish on his face. "What happened?"

"He's gone, Katherine. He's gone." His arms snapped around her and his voice caught on the last word as he buried his face into her shoulder and sobbed as if his heart were breaking. Kat had to take deep breaths before her own tears overcame her. She stroked up and down his back, offering what little comfort she could.

It was impossible to say how long they remained there. The most poignant thing Kat saw as she looked around was a worn leather cat collar sitting on the dining table. A cat collar with no owner. Devlin finally lifted his head, swiping the wetness from his face. "I'm sorry."

She led him to the sofa and sat beside him. "You never have to apologise to me. What happened?"

He brushed the hair back from her face with a hand that shook. "I fed the three of them when I got home, that's when I sent the photo, then I crashed out for a few hours. I was so tired I could barely think. Othello was on the pillow next to me, I remember the sound of his purring and the warmth of his fur." His voice cracked for a moment. "When I woke up, he wasn't on the bed. I checked his favourite spot outside and saw him curled up." He sucked in a shaky breath. "The sun was shining so I left him there. When I was about to leave for the school, I went out to give him a last head rub, but he didn't respond."

Kat swallowed her tears and let him speak.

"I brought him inside. He... he was limp in my arms. The vets came straight away after I called them, but it was too late. He'd just... slipped away." Dev's voice broke and fresh tears flowed. "They checked him for bites or other injuries but said they couldn't find anything. It was if his heart just stopped. He was nineteen, Kat, that's a good age for a cat. At his last annual check-up, they said he'd lost some weight and his kidney function had decreased. They said there would probably come a time when we'd have to… assess his quality of life. I dreaded that, dreading having to make such a horrible decision. Perhaps Othello knew that. Perhaps he decided for me." He broke off at that point, unable to continue. Kat just held him until he regained control and wiped the tears away. "Sorry."

"I told you, you need never apologise to me for being human, for mourning someone you loved. I know what you're feeling, Devlin."

"He was my cat. You lost your parents."

"Do you think that matters to me? Do you really think I'd think less of you for *who* you're grieving?"

He kissed her, a poignantly simple brush of lips. "I didn't even ask about your exam."

"I was awesome." She spoke the words, words that would end her future at Perdies without regret.

"I knew you would be." He gathered her close.

Further words weren't necessary. How many people had tried to comfort her with meaningless platitudes years ago? How many of them had failed? Kat put her hand to his chest, listening to the rapid thump of his heartbeat.

Memories flickered in his eyes. Kat gave him the time he needed, following whatever path he needed to go down. The phone rang at some point. Devlin let it go to message. When he finally talked, she listened.

"I was nine years old when I found him, half drowned huddled next to a storm drain. He meowed as I walked past, a pitiful sound, otherwise I'd never have seen him, he was so filthy. We'd had a week of rain prior to that, horrible weather. God knows where he came from, or how long he'd been there. He was shivering so much, I tucked him inside my jacket and ran all the way home. I remember Mum cooked up some chicken mince for him to eat. He wolfed it down so fast I thought he would be sick." Devlin paused, his chest rising and falling with his breaths. "For the rest of his life, he loved being cuddled. And he loved the sunshine, maybe because he always remembered being cold."

Kat didn't try to hide the tears streaming down her cheeks. She had to clear her throat before she could talk. "He was your first opera cat."

A tight laugh escaped him, with just a trace of genuine humour. "Not opera, it was from the book. I'd snuck it out of the library because it sounded exciting, and started reading it on the school bus, but gave up and tucked it into my jacket pocket because it was so bloody violent. The jig was up once the pages got wet and dirty from Othello's fur, the library even made me pay a fine, plus they freaked out because I was *way* too young to be reading it. After all the drama that book created, Othello's name seemed appropriate."

"You mean without all that, Evita and Carmen could have been plain old Sue and Karen?"

"Do I sound like an idiot? Crazy cat man?" His voice was stronger, although still thick with sadness.

"Remember I *like* crazy cat men."

"Evita and Carmen prowled around the house for hours after the vets took him away earlier. I swear they were looking for him. I'll spread his ashes on his favourite spot once they return them. I think he would have liked that. He was special, Katherine.

There was a bond between us, and do you know why? I think he chose me. Who knows how many people walked past that drain before I did. Othello called out to me, he chose me. That made us special. When I was a kid, I'd tell him all my secrets, all my dreams."

The honest confession, so heartfelt, resonated with her on a bone deep level.

"I've been away so much these last few months, and yet I got to say goodbye. Do you think he knew? He was so affectionate when I got home, curled up against me, purring like a demon." At her shaky inhale of breath, Dev stroked her hair. "I'm sorry, I'm upsetting you."

"Only in a good way."

With their bodies entwined, time slipped away. The sun weaved its way through the window, cocooning them in its warmth. "Thank you for being here." He brushed his lips over hers again with exquisite gentleness. The moment was spoilt by the shrill of the landline, followed moments later by the echo of a cell phone vibrating on some hard surface.

Devlin's grin held a hint of its usual mischief. "Why are people always interrupting us at inopportune moments?"

"That's what happens when you're a very important person."

He stirred, trying to sit up. "I'll make some tea."

Kat tried to hold him in place, knowing all too well what was about to happen. "Is tea your answer to everything?"

"It's a multi-function problem solver, from curing hangovers to soothing singers—" Kat saw the apology in his eyes. "Christ, what must you think of me? I haven't even asked for details of the exam. Tell me everything?" This time he sat up, putting both hands on her face. "Wait, before you tell me, let me say something. If it doesn't work out—and I'm sure you *were* awesome—but if it doesn't work out, promise me you'll let me write you a reference, to any other music school in the country. Preferably within ten miles of where we are right now. Because, I sure as hell don't want you moving across state lines. I'd miss you way too much."

The seconds stretched out until Dev gave her a strange look. "Katherine?"

"I bought you something," she avoided his eyes and rushed to the car, coming back with the gift bag.

When he pulled out the cane, a myriad of emotions crossed his face, too many to catch.

She took it from his hands and extended it to its full length. "I checked with the airports. It's plane compliant. You can't be Perdie without a Perdies cane."

His voice was husky. "Katherine. It's beautiful. It's perfect." He stroked the carved feline face. "It looks like him, don't you think? A fitting monument to someone very special to me."

Moment of truth time.

Kat sucked in a breath. "I need to tell you something about the exam. Don't freak out."

"Why would I?"

"It was at two thirty."

For a heartbeat, he did nothing, until the implications of her words reached him. Devlin shot off the sofa in one smooth move. "*What?* What's the time? Where's my phone? Where's my bloody phone." He patted his trousers, searching for it. Kat could see the cell sitting on the countertop. She didn't need him to tell her what time it was, she could tell from the change of light outside, *and* there was the large wall clock right in front of her.

He finally remembered its looming presence, and spun to face it. "It's, its…"

"Ten past six. Yes, I can see that."

"Wait? What time did you get here?" The *full* ramifications sunk in as the colour drained from his flushed cheeks. "I'll ring the committee."

Kat scrambled from the sofa, as he lunged for his cell and dialled "Don't you dare!"

The look on his face was as tortured as when she'd arrived. "You didn't just miss the exam. You missed it because of *me*."

"I chose to miss it. Don't ruin it. Don't take control of something I can't." She plucked the phone from his fingers and tossed it to the sofa. "I made the choice. It was mine to take and I chose you. 'Permission to fail', remember? If it makes you feel better, I'll accept your letter of recommendation. See? You're rubbing off on me." She tried to lighten the fraught atmosphere with a smile.

Devlin's arms snapped around her for the second time that day. "Tell me this isn't happening?"

"Happened, past tense. There's nothing you can do about it now."

"There *has* to be. It can't end like this."

"Please, Devlin, let it go. I'm here, I want to be here."

He pressed his lips to her, in a kiss laden with poignant emotion.

"Wait." He released her, only to hold her at arm's length. "Wait."

"Wait for what?"

"A chance, a slim one, but a chance."

"You're not making sense."

"No time to explain. Time is of the essence." He grabbed the new Perdies cane from the sofa and handed it to her, before almost pushing her towards the back of the town house and into the connecting garage.

"Where are we going?"

"To a pub."

"I'm not in a drinking mood."

"Neither am I, but you know who will be? The admissions committee."

"How do you know?" Her question was punctuated with pauses as Devlin hauled open the car door and lifted her inside.

"The committee are sticklers for routine and creatures of habit. They *always* go for drinks after final evaluations, and always to the same place. I've teased them about it in the past, told them to mix it up a bit. Now I'm grateful."

"What if they mix it up this year?"

"Let's hope they don't."

Kat scrubbed at a stain on her trousers caused by an overfull cup of juice. Her T-shirt was wrinkled from lying on Devlin's couch. Her hair was a tangled mess. Even her shoes were old and grungy, worn for comfort not style. "I'm not ready."

"Katherine, my love. You've been ready for this your entire life."

Devlin looked exhausted, the shadows under his eyes emphasizing the pallor of his cheeks. Even without the stress of Othello's death, he'd been running himself ragged for weeks. She reached out a hand to touch his face. "This isn't right. I wanted to be there for you."

He took one hand off the wheel to capture her fingers, pressing them to his lips. "You were. Now it's *my* turn."

The journey was relatively short. His hands were tight on the wheel and Kat didn't want to ruin his already splintered concentration. He pulled into a rear car park of a trendy tavern on the South Perth foreshore. Leaning across the seat, her hauled her close for a lightning-fast kiss. "I'll park. Ask at the desk, the table reservation will be under Perdies."

"Okay. Wait, why do I have the cane?"

"For luck."

She clutched the cool brass in her hands and slid from the car. "You need to go."

"No way. I'm not leaving you here alone."

"I'll catch a cab and ring you later."

"Do you have your bag?"

No, she didn't. Her bag, and everything in it, including her phone *and* her sheet music, was at Devlin's house. Not to mention the carefully prepared clothing ensemble at the school. Talk about unprepared. "You realise this about sums up my entire Perdies experience so far. *Fine*, I'll go in. You stay in the car. Promise me."

"I promise."

"Don't hover."

"I give you my word. Will you please *move*?"

Kat straightened the shirt and smoothed a hand down her trousers, a fruitless task.

At least I'm not dressed as a stewardess.

The wry thought ended in a strangled laugh borne of nerves, not humour, that lodged in her throat. Could there be a more inappropriate situation to have a giggle fit?

She made her way to the main entrance just as a group of people spilled out from it, chatting together, three men and three women. All were impeccably dressed, and easily recognisable as formidable figures within the music industry. Kat's footsteps slowed, then stopped as her stomach tied itself in knots.

Either this was a weird coincidence, or Devlin had failed to mention the distinguished calibre of his admissions committee. "Excuse me."

"Yes?" A former conductor of the state's symphony orchestra glanced in her direction.

"My name is Katherine Grant, a Perdies probation student. I'm on your list for today."

"You *were*, Miss Grant, more than four hours ago."

Wow, tough crowd.

"I know I'm late."

He put up his hand. "Perdies is an exclusive music establishment, ranked one of the highest in the country. Because of this, the submission applications number in the hundreds each semester."

"I'm aware of that."

"Are you also aware of our strict criteria regarding attendance and punctuality for our probationary students?"

Very tough crowd.

"I am."

"And yet, you missed your final exam altogether, leaving with no explanation."

"Someone I care about with all my heart needed me. I'm not excusing my behaviour, simply giving you a reason for it."

There was a pause, and a few more exchanged glances. If they wanted more details, too bad, Devlin's grief was not for public consumption.

A second woman, a retired opera singer famous in the 1970s for her soaring arias, tapped him on the arm. "In our reports, Katherine received the highest praise from all her teachers. You have to agree her marks for attendance and for performance were exemplary."

Mr. Orchestra wasn't so easily swayed. "Second chances are not part of our standard operating procedure."

"Perhaps this could be an exception?"

"Are you suggesting we conduct our final exam in a public carpark?"

"Let me sing." Kat blurted the words out, interrupting their debate.

All eyes turned in her direction. "Now?"

"Why not? Five minutes of your time is all I'm asking. Mr. Perdie said the college is about music, and students who have the determination to learn. I love music, and I'm stubbornly determined, ask anyone. Please, let me sing, right here, right now."

The opera singer gave her an appraising look. "Without musical accompaniment?"

"I've done it before, many times."

"You've chosen a song?"

"Yes."

"Very well." This from the conductor. "In the interest of fairness, we'll give you a couple of minutes to prepare." They turned away from her to talk in low tones, their heads bent together.

Kat wiped her damp palms on her trousers. This was fine. She'd practiced the French ballad for hours, over and over until she was word perfect.

Just think of it as a singing telegram.

Devlin would laugh out loud when she told him that. Kat peered into the distance, trying to pick out his car. The parking area was full. Maybe he'd gone someplace else.

A flurry of air swirled the fallen leaves around her feet. The lamplight flickered above her as she stood in the darkness.

No. He was here, listening, she was certain of it. Standing somewhere nearby, offering silent support and encouragement, despite his grief, the sadness in his heart, and the memories of his beloved pet so close to the surface. She stroked the head of the cane, tracing her fingers over the feline features.

It looks like him, don't you think?

He always loved the sunshine.

I'd tell him all my secrets. All my dreams.

Memories. As light bulb moments went, it was a biggie. A world shattering, possibly life changing revelation of epic proportions.

And I'm having it in a carpark.

Whatever, it wasn't as if life had gone smoothly up to this point. What was another wrinkle? Kat only knew, with absolute conviction, with complete and utter certainty, that the French balled was all wrong.

There was only one song she needed to sing tonight. A song about sadness and loss, about love and life and... memories.

"I'm ready."

"Very well, Miss Grant. Please begin."

"I'm going to perform *Memory*, from *Cats*."

A blind man could have seen their disappointment; it hung in the air with a palpable presence. Kat could see it in their faces. She could feel the disinterest radiating from them in waves.

She tuned all of that out. Obsessing would distract from her performance, and steal the passion from her words. Drawing in a deep breath right to the limit of her lungs, Kat called up the opening bars of the music, counted them out in her mind, then began to sing. She sang from the heart, from a place deep within her soul. She sang for the love and loss of her parents, for the years with them she'd never get to experience. She sang for all the precious childhood memories no one could take away from her. Most of all, Kat sang for Devlin, for his own loss, *his* childhood memories of his treasured friend.

To heal his pain and his sadness, she gave him her voice, and her heart.

The very last note hitched, just a fraction, as emotion tightened her throat, but it rang true, and lingered in the air.

Blinking the world back into focus, Kat turned to the six-member committee. “Thank you for the opportunity. I can’t tell you how much it means to me, but I have to go.”

“Go?” The single word was spoken in unison.

“Someone needs me. I have to get back to him. Thank you again.” Kat threw the final words over her shoulder. She was already running, searching.

Where are you, Devlin?

He stepped out from behind the moonlit dappled tree and caught her in his arms, lifting her high off the ground. His crushing embrace was so tight around her, she could barely breathe.

“Why? Why would you do that?” His voice was hoarse and strained.

“You know why.”

“You’re crazy, *crazy*.”

“Hey, that’s your official tag, not mine.”

“This was your one chance.”

“Yeah, it was. At least say you liked it.”

"Katherine." Her name of his lips held a world of emotion.

Uncontrolled shivers raked Kat's body as adrenaline and emotion warred for control. This incredible man and his incredible music schools around Australia were going to make so many dreams come true, change *so* many lives. So what if hers wasn't destined to be one of them? That didn't matter right now, because the murmured words he was repeating over and over like a mantra were a beautiful symphony.

"I love you. I love you. I love you."

Chapter Nine

SHE WOKE ALONE THE next morning. They'd talked throughout the night, talked, and finally made love as the dawn broke.

"Hi." Devlin stood in the doorway dressed only in sweat pants, holding two glasses of juice.

Kat propped herself higher on the pillows. "You should be in bed. I was going to make you breakfast." Dark shadows were still visible under his eyes.

"I am allowed to spoil you sometimes, my sweet." His smile took some of the fatigue from his features.

Instead of handing her the glass, he put both on the bedside table, and climbed back into bed, pulling her close. Kat wasn't about to complain. Instead she held him, sharing in his sadness, comforting him as much as she could.

Devlin touched the empty pillow next to her. "I'm going to miss him for a long time."

"I know, and that's okay."

"Thank you, for being here."

"Where else would I be?" She kissed him. "Was that your phone I heard?"

"It was. Mum was reminding me I need to pick them up at the airport later tonight. *Much* later, it seems, their flight out of Dubai is delayed."

Kat entwined her fingers with his. "Can I ask you something?"

"Of course."

"You seem close to your family and yet you hardly talk about them, and there are no photos anywhere."

He pressed his lips to her forehead. "We are close, ridiculously close, and it's why I kept quiet. How could I rub that lifelong family unity in your face knowing it was taken from you?"

The simple honesty touched her more than she could say.

He continued. "As for the photos, there's an art gallery's worth propped up in the spare bedroom. A comprehensive pictorial storyboard of Jones family life. All I need is to find time to bang some nails in the damn walls."

She wriggled against him. "I can fix that for you. I've done so many DIY repairs at my place, I'm the hammer queen."

"I'll take you up on that offer. And I'll show you the pictures after breakfast... better still, come with me to the airport tonight and you can meet them in person. Mum will adore you, as will the demon twins."

Kat's fingers stilled on his skin. "Twins?"

"My younger brothers. I warn you, they'll take a while to get used to, especially as they're identical and no one can tell them apart and they pretty much define the word mischief, but you'll learn to love them I promise—Katherine? Where are you going?"

Twins. Identical twins.

She scrambled from the bed while he was still talking, almost falling over her own feet in her haste. Her stumbling steps carried her along the short corridor to the spare room. She sunk to her knees and shifted a few of the stacked picture frames leaning against the wall, looking, searching…

"Katherine?" Devlin's tone had a worried edge as he crouched beside her.

She didn't need to ask him the question hovering on her lips. The evidence was staring her in the face, literally. Two smiling familiar faces. Identical faces. "John and Jason."

His surprise was clear. "Wait, you know the twins?"

It all clicked into place, finally, all the pieces coming together in her mind. It had been there *all* along.

"Do you have brothers?" Devlin had said that to her on the first morning they'd met.

"Our brother's cool."

"Super cool. I mean, really, really cool. He's promised to buy us a car."

So many clues, and she hadn't picked up on a single one.

Devlin drew her attention back to him with his hand on her cheek. "Katherine?"

Kat cleared her throat. "When the agency rang me about the telegram, your telegram, they insisted I do it. It had to be me, I never understood why."

"You were the best?"

"Guess again. Where do I work, Devlin? When I'm not at Perdics."

"A café."

"Which café."

"I... I'm sorry, it was on your resume, I don't remember the name. Is it important?"

"The name, probably not. The location, yeah. It's on the university grounds."

She could see the dawning comprehension in his eyes. "Oh God." Devlin yanked her into his arms. "Oh God, this is bad, isn't it? It's bad."

It was planned. It was *all* planned. Kat closed her eyes against the familiar rush of unwelcome sensations coming at her in waves, stemming from the parts of her life she resented with every fibre of her being. Control. Interference. Special Treatment. Lack of choice.

Devlin spoke. "I need you to listen to me, can you do that? Before you freak out and run, because that's what you want to do right now, right? And you know we've been here before and frankly neither of us are dressed for a mad dash down the street, so I want you to give me two minutes and listen, okay?"

"Okay." He was holding her so tight her words were muffled against his bare chest.

"Good. There are four things you need to know about the twins. First, as you've correctly ascertained, they're my brothers. Second, they're insanely curious and insanely intelligent. Finally, they're incurable romantics, and passionate about family."

"That's three. What's the fourth thing?"

"They've always wanted a sister."

Kat opened and closed her mouth a few times.

"You just said the agency gave you the birthday assignment that landed you on my doorstep. *You* specifically."

"Yes."

"I'm guessing my brothers knew about your singing, and your telegram job?"

"My love of singing, yes. The job, I honestly can't remember. I may have mentioned it once."

"Trust me, once is all they need. Did I mention the off the charts IQ? Did they know you'd applied to Perdies?"

"No. I only told them after I got accepted."

His breath came out in a rush. "Thank God for that."

"Why?"

"Because it means we have a chance."

Kat tried to weave her way through her tangled thoughts. "Is this conversation going to get less confusing at any point?"

He moved his hands from her shoulders to her face. "You're freaking out because you think they planned this."

"They *did* plan this. *All* of it."

"Think for a moment. If John and Jason had said, 'hey, my brother runs a prestigious music school, should we put in a good word for you?' what would you have done?"

"I would have said no."

"Exactly. And if they'd come to me and said 'hey, there's this woman we know who has a great voice, want to meet her?' *I* would have said no. My brothers, therefore, took a more circular route."

"They put us together."

"No wonder they got me so drunk the night before my birthday, they needed me to be at home the following morning."

Warring emotions fought for control in Kat's mind. "They wanted me at Perdies?"

"If I know the twins, and trust me, I do, this has *nothing* to do with the school. John and Jason wanted you *here*, in my arms, and as part of the family. Prepare yourself for some news, my sweet. We've been officially match-maked."

The only word Kat could think of was, "Oh."

"We've been romantically thrown together by two nineteen-year-olds using a pop song and a black marker pen because they knew we'd be perfect for each other."

"Oh."

"This wasn't about control, Katherine, or about special treatment at Perdies. My brothers wanted us to meet, so we could fall in love." He waited for a few seconds before speaking again. "How is this sitting with you?"

He knew. He knew, and he understood. "It's a lot to take in. I'm not entirely sure."

"Can I kiss you while you decide? Or should I put my running shoes on? Because I'm up for a dash down the street if that's what you need. Heck, I'll do it shirtless and shoeless if you want me to."

"Kissing will work."

"Good."

His lips were a lifeboat she clung to in a sea of uncertainty and she focused on that. Devlin's kiss. Devlin's arms wrapped around her. Devlin's body pressed to hers.

After several minutes, or possibly years, he pulled back. "Conclusions?"

She gathered her thoughts for long minutes. Control. Interference. Lack of choice. She'd run from those elements of her life for years. And yet, here she was, caught in the middle of a life planned by someone else. It represented *everything* she'd fought so hard against.

Except... Devlin was right. This time it wasn't about control, or interference. Her knee jerk reaction was coming from the past. A past she *had* moved on from. She adored Devlin's brothers. Katherine pictured their faces in the café, their eyes shining when they talked about Devlin. Their friendship and understanding when she'd talked about losing her parents.

"If I had brothers, I'd like them to be just like you."

"Do you mean that?"

They'd done it for love.

Love. Like all the best songs ever written, it all circled back to love. "After careful consideration, it seems a shame for all the twin's efforts to go to waste."

"You mean we're still dating?"

She threw him a wry look. "What are we, twelve?"

"Sorry, I panicked."

His honest answer made her smile, then laugh, with a lightness in her heart.

He gave her a strange look as if confused by her unexpected reaction. Kat pulled back until Devlin released her, and took several deep breaths. "Here's a thought."

"I'm listening."

"What if we don't tell them their plan worked?"

A grin replaced the wariness on his face. "That would drive them crazy."

"I know."

"How long should we keep up the charade?"

Kat pretended to give the matter serious thought. "I think their 40th birthday should suffice."

"Yep, I'm sure that's doable." He nodded in serious agreement, even as mischief danced in his eyes.

"Of course, once we have a couple of kids, they might twig to the truth."

One brow rose in question. “Was that a proposal of marriage, Katherine?”

She traced a finger along his bare chest. “I prefer to think of it as a not, *not* a proposal, rather something to be revisited at a later date.”

He moved close, until his lips were just hovering over hers. “You should know, I fully intend accepting your not, *not* a proposal and look forward to revisiting the subject at a future time of your choosing.”

“Good.”

“You know I love you, right?”

“You have made that clear.”

“It helps if you say it back, especially as we’re almost not, *not* engaged.”

Her choice. Her life. Her love. Her family. The universe—and two lovable, romantically inclined twins—had given her a new life, a future she’d never ever dreamed of, and she was *not* about to let it get away.

She wrapped her arms around his neck. “You are the music in my soul, Devlin Sebastian Perdie Jones, and, yes, I love you, with all my heart.”

Chapter Ten

LATER

DEV FLOPPED INTO HIS office chair and dialled the school. Jules answered on the first ring.

"Hi, boss, why are you calling, it's your birthday, remember? You're supposed to be having a day off."

"I am, but I've just seen the probation application numbers. Are these right?"

"Sure are. We're up thirty percent in Adelaide and thirty five percent in Sydney. Not to mention the soaring numbers in Perth. You will need a fourth school at this rate. By the way, I'm giving myself another pay rise, and hiring another assistant."

"Fine by me."

"It's a *big* pay rise."

"Even better."

"One last thing. *People Magazine* rang, asking for an interview. They're planning an article called, 'The man behind the famous Perdies cane.'"

Dev glanced at the aforementioned item, propped up next to the doorway. "Tell them thanks, but no thanks."

He checked the latest emails after hanging up. Tom had sent an invite to his debut concert with a newly formed wind quartet, and Ava had forwarded photos from her latest performance in Germany. Katherine would be thrilled with their news. The intercom buzzed, and kept buzzing. He wheeled his chair backwards and hit the button. "Yes?"

"I'm a tiger, I'm a tiger..."

Surrendering to laughter, and the familiar surge of desire Katherine's singing always created, he kept the tone of his voice serious. "Excuse me. I believe you have the wrong house."

"Very funny. Let me in before my arms break."

Dev bounded down the stairs, taking them two at a time, and flung open the door.

"Did you forget your key again?"

"I ran out of hands. I couldn't reach it," she shoved three large grocery bags in his direction.

He took them, almost dislocating his shoulders from the weight. "Sweetheart, we're having a dinner party for five people, not fifty."

"I know that. Hold on, I'll get the rest," she headed back to the car.

"Rest? How much stuff did you *buy*?"

"Birthday parties require a lot of food. You know the twins eat enough for ten." She squeezed past him in the doorway juggling several more bags, pressing a kiss to his mouth in passing.

"You were gone for hours. I thought you'd left me."

"Never. I had to make a detour for extra supplies."

He eyed the grocery hoard with disappointment. "More food? When I heard your sexy voice, I thought I was in for another birthday telegram. Visions of black leotards and flirty flight attendants are running though my head."

"I'm saving *that* present for when we're alone." Katherine blew him another kiss as she dumped the bags on the counter.

He curled his hands around her hips, pulling her closer. "To hell with family. They can visit tomorrow."

"Tomorrow isn't your birthday." Despite her laughing protests, she offered no resistance when he nudged aside her hair to lay kisses on her neck.

"Mum will understand, I promise. Sing *'I'm a Tiger for me'*. Go up a key, I want to test your range."

Her chin kicked skywards, as he knew it would. "You only get to boss your students around. I'm your wife, *and* I graduated Perdies with top honours, despite auditioning in a car park."

Dev pursed his lips in thought. "I think you've mentioned that a *few* times in the last three years. I vaguely remember you incorporated it into our wedding vows."

Katherine snaked her arms around his neck. "Could you start peeling vegetables?"

"Is there any chance that's a euphemism for something sexy?"

"No."

"Damn."

"Do you want to serve your family takeaway? We're running out of time."

"In that case, what difference will five more minutes make, after all, it *is* my birthday." He lowered his mouth to hers.

"Aargh I'm blind, *blind*." Dev broke off the kiss with reluctance at the sound of John's tortured tone.

"Are they naked again? I bet they're naked again." Jason was two steps behind his twin, fumbling his way into the house with his hand covering his eyes.

Dev planted his hands on his hips. "Yes, well you wouldn't keep discovering us naked if you learnt how to *knock*."

"Please stop aggravating your brother." Madeline Jones nudged her youngest sons out of the way and gave Katherine a kiss on the cheek which was returned with love and affection. "Hello darling, happy birthday. In the twins' defence, the front door was wide open. If you want to start working on my first grandchild, perhaps you should keep it closed."

Dev gave her a rueful look. "You could be on your way to that grandchild right now, if you'd waited another half an hour."

"Devlin." Katherine nudged him in the ribs, a blush rising on her cheeks.

"We got you a gift." This from Jason.

"A special gift." John's echo was a millisecond after his brother, as usual.

"You're going to love it."

"Really love it."

"Are you going to give it to him?"

"I thought you had it."

"*You* were supposed to get it out of the car."

"No, I wasn't."

"You totally were."

They disappeared back out the door in a tangle of limbs, still arguing.

Dev shook his head and kissed his mother. "They're twenty-two. When are they going to actually grow up?"

She patted his cheek. "One day, darling, but not today."

The twins returned a minute later holding a wicker basket between them. They lifted out an object wrapped in a towel and laid it with great care on the sofa. The ginger kitten blinked and meowed, the timid sound going straight to Dev's heart. He dropped to his knees, soothing its cries with gentle strokes along its dirty fur. "It's okay, little one, no one's going to hurt you."

"Gino found it outside the café early this morning."

"He told us when we went in for coffee before class."

"He was looking for the number of an animal rescue centre."

"We told him to wait until we showed you."

"We know you said you didn't want another cat."

"You've said that *heaps* of times."

"But he needs you."

"Like, really totally needs you."

The twins were still talking when Katherine sat down beside him, resting her head on his shoulder.

Carmen leapt on the sofa, and gave the kitten a thorough sniff. After a moment's hesitation, she began washing its head with ruthless efficiency. The new arrival closed its eyes in bliss; its loud purr echoing through the house. Evita refused to be left out. She joined the melee, and within seconds the kitten was being groomed at both ends, and appeared happy at the prospect.

Jason spoke up. "We think it's a boy, but he isn't a replacement for Othello. You know we'd never do that."

"But he was alone and scared. So, we thought he belonged here." This from John.

"And it's your birthday."

Dev picked the kitten up. It snuggled into his neck, just as Othello had always done, and he had to take a breath as a barrage of powerful emotions hit him.

Madeline clapped her hands at the hovering twins. "Come on, you two, let your brother and sister-in-law have some peace and quiet. You can peel vegetables with me. It about time you learnt how to look after yourselves. You do know you can't live at home, or stay at university forever, right?"

Her suggestion was met with a chorus of groans.

"You're cruel, Mum,"

"Super cruel."

"Totally cruel."

Dev settled on the sofa, the kitten still purring against his skin. Katherine pressed a kiss to his cheek. "Are you okay?"

"You know what? I think I am. How do you feel about expanding the feline household back to three?"

"Do you even have to ask? And it seems you already have full approval from the masses." She gestured to the other cats. On cue, Carmen let out a disgruntled meow. Evita fixed him with a silent glare.

Dev rolled his eyes at both of them. "Excuse me, I get first cuddles. You can wash the newbie later."

"What about a name? I'm guessing you'll want something operatic."

"Maybe it's time for a change of old habits. What does the tabby pattern remind you of? I'll give you a clue, you *didn't* have them on your leotard."

Her smile grew, and memories danced in her eyes. "As you know…it *is* a tradition to have tigers on your birthday."

"Exactly." Dev tickled the new household member under the chin. "Hello, Tiger, welcome to your new home. I hope you are a boy, I'm outnumbered by women in this house." Tiger head-butted him in the chin with surprising strength, causing his teeth to come together with a painful snap.

"Ouch, my poor Devlin." Katherine's laughter caressed his soul like a kiss.

"Do you have any idea how much I love you."

"I have a rough idea. You may have mentioned it once or twice. Is this the best birthday ever?"

"Second best."

"Do I make it into the top five at least?"

"Top of the list, my life and my world, my sweet, always."

Surrounded by family, human and cats, Dev gave thanks for his amazing life. He and Katherine had a lifetime ahead. Days, months, years, hopefully *decades*, of love, laughter, and memories. But, if she'd taught him anything, it was that life was a series of moments, and every one had to be treasured. Katherine was his life, and every single moment with her was priceless.

No. It was even better than that.

It was purrfect.

THE END

Acknowledgements

To music genius Andrew Lloyd Webber and lyricists Trevor Nunn and Richard Stilgoe, for creating the musical, Cats. And to poet T.S. Eliot, who was the inspiration.

My first memory (no pun intended) of the song, Memory, is from the Royal Variety Performance in 1981. Andrew Lloyd Webber played piano, and Elaine Paige sung. I was blown away by the power and emotion of the song.

When I was lucky enough to attend the live theatrical version of Cats in Australia in 1985, and saw on stage the full context of the song, an older cat nearing the end of her life, recalling her youth and beauty from long ago, I was reduced to tears and almost had to leave the theatre!

The song has always been special to me. The Barbra Streisand version, also released in 1981, was Mums favourite. She used to play it all the time and hum along to the music as she cooked.

I could never have guessed back then that this music would form the emotional heart of a Romantic Comedy I wrote myself.

Obviously I couldn't use song lyrics in the book because of copyright, but if you're unfamiliar with the song, I encourage you to listen to it, and I hope it resonates with you as much as it always has with me, and with the characters in this book.

Carolyn Wren

Playlist

Just for fun, here are the musical references mentioned in Purr-Fect Pitch.

I'm A Tiger – Lulu

What's New Pussycat – Tom Jones

Come Fly With Me – Frank Sinatra

Stand By Your Man – Tammy Wynette

Hopelessly Devoted To You – Olivia Newton-John

Les Trois Cloche – Tina Arena

Memory – Eileen Paige (or the Barbra Streisand version)

Moonlight Sonata – Beethoven
Sonata no. 9 – Mozart
Polonaise in A Flat Major – Chopin
Liebestraum– Franz Liszt
The Celebrated Chop Waltz (Also known as Chopsticks in its simplified form) – Euphemia Allan (under the pen name of Arthur de Lulli)

Also by

Carolyn Wren

Paranormal

Stolen Memory Bonded Memory Silent Memory

Secret Memory Broken Memory Sacred Memory

Paranormal Erotic Romance

Ghosts of Grace Cottage

Multi Award Winning Romantic Suspense

CrossFire A Note of Desire A Passion in Flames

A Glitter of Obsession An Emotion In Chains

A Danger of Longing To Adore an Enemy A Memory of Love

Award Winning Romantic Comedy

Purr-Fect Pitch

For other book titles go to www.carolynwren.com

About The Author

Carolyn Wren was born just outside of London and moved with her family to Western Australia when she was four. They returned to England when she was eight and came back again when she was eleven, all by cruise ship, meaning Carolyn had traversed most of the words oceans before she became a teenager. The resulting passion for travel has never left her.

After a working life in the finance sector, Carolyn began writing fiction in 2009, for fun. She won the very first writing contest she entered which gave her the incentive to keep going. Her award tally so far is 10 wins and 24 finalist placings from all around the world. The trophies and certificates are displayed with a great deal of pride.

She's a proud member of the Romance Writers of Australia, Australian Society of New Zealand. Australian Society of Authors and the Australian Romance Readers Association.

Carolyn doesn't like to limit herself to one genre, preferring to let her characters take control. The resulting stories can range from light-hearted comedic contemporary through to sexy, action packed romantic suspense and emotion driven urban fantasy. Because she's a true romantic at heart, one thing remains constant in all her books, she loves a happy ending.

If you'd like to know more about Carolyn, you can connect with her on the following links. She happily admits to being hopeless at social media, but she does check her messages.

www.carolynwren.com

https///www.facebook.com.carolynwrenauthor

www.ingramcontent.com/pod-product-compliance
Lightning Source LLC
Chambersburg PA
CBHW022132050726
47590CB00002B/513
* 9 7 8 1 7 6 4 3 1 8 1 5 0 *